The Crow Dark Sea
Book I: The Heretic

Duncan Bourne is a UK writer, artist and illustrator. His artwork has appeared in a diverse range of media, books and magazines. He has written songs celebrating little known tales from local history. He has written for various magazines and **Book 1: The Heretic** is the first part of **The Crow Dark Sea** trilogy.

His first novel, **The Dark Heart**, the story of Kazi and Jay is available from Amazon.

The Crow Dark Sea
Book I: The Heretic

Duncan Bourne

Published by Hunters Path 2024

The Crow Dark Sea
Book I: The Heretic
copyright © 2024 Duncan Bourne

All rights reserved. This book or any portion thereof may not be reproduced or used in any manner whatsoever without the express written permission of the copyright owner except for the use of brief quotations in a book review.

First Edition

ISBN 978-1-7399265-1-9

Published by Hunters Path

Dedicated to:

my parents, Doreen and David Bourne.

With many thanks to the Renegade Writers, my wife, Michèle and other friends for their invaluable feedback and to Cathy Woodhead for her invaluable proof-reading.

The crow dark sea.
Never ending, ever changing.
Casts brief stories on the shore
To be read awhile and then erased.
The imprint of our lives wiped clean
Like waves over sand

From "Yātrā, the travels and teachings of Dharmajara" (430 BCE)

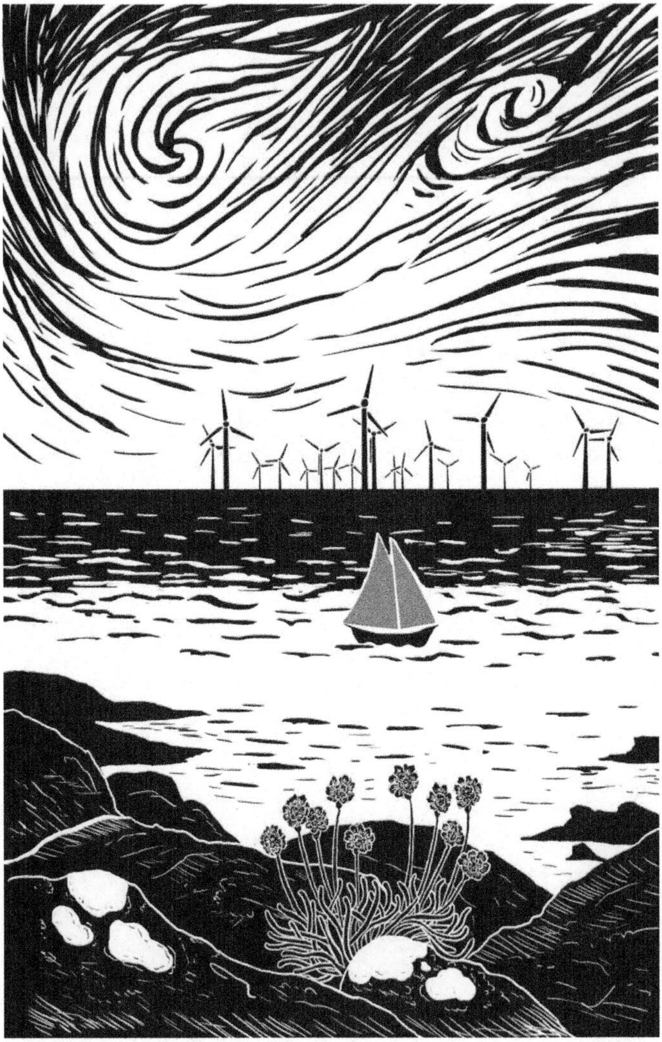

Part 1: Family Politics

My father used to say:
"Four things govern life and death, your actions, the actions of those around you, the environment and time.
And the greatest of these is time.
For if the other three don't get you time eventually will."

From "The collected sayings of Mathew Kaga Vakta." (3057)

Chapter 1 – Above an Angry Sea

Scabbed with suppurating rust, like old blood, the army of broken wind turbines pierced the haze of the Eirish Sea. I, Mathew Pembrock, son of Lord Gruffydd, crossed myself against their ancient evil and focused my gaze on the small boat, its red sail full as it skimmed the glistening waves towards harbour at New Porth Clais. It was the year 2949 and I was twenty-one.

"So, the heretic's released from quarantine then?" a cultured voice behind me quipped with Gaelic lilt.

I turned too quick on the slick, black rocks and stumbling almost fell to the foaming waves. "Holy Jay'n'Kazi, Mog! Must you come upon me like a ghost in the night?"

Poised above me, bare feet planted firmly on the salt-stained ridge, cousin Morag grinned and gestured towards the boat. "Do you know why he's a heretic?"

Her embroidered skirt, tied at the thigh, exposed too much leg for my youthful prudishness. My own attire reflected a respectable military style.

"No," I said. "But Bishop Ellis has called for his arrest the moment he strikes land."

"Well Bishop Ellis will be disappointed. Your father has made it perfectly clear he will be black furious if the Examiners so much as lay a finger on the man."

"I know and it blows cold across me." Though I often questioned the motives of the Brethon Church, I was ever a true believer, for who would incur the wrath of the Cigfrân? "What can Da want with a renegade priest?" I wondered aloud.

"May as well ask the gulls. He doesn't confide in me." Morag brushed a strand of windblown black hair from her pale face. Too pale I thought.

"Are you ill?" I asked.

"A little sickness. I swear last night's fish was off." Though barefoot, she was high born and wore a shirt of good Welsh linen and her fine burgundy leather waistcoat bore testament to a privileged life. Descending the rocks, Morag reached out to touch the still tender bruise on my face, her expression half mocking half concerned.

I flinched away from her touch and the sour memory of acquiring it. "Should you not be preparing for Evening Service, Mog?"

Her lips parted in a broad grin. "Shouldn't you? You're not in the Militia now you know."

Annoyed at the reminder of my defunct career, I pointed to her feet. "Does Da know you go barefoot like a common peasant?"

Morag laughed, bright as the sunlit waves. "The day's too hot for shoes. Your father can rage all he wants."

"What he wants is children. He's pushing me to marry some Eirish chief's daughter. Fifteen years old can you believe? And we've never even met."

"Is she strong? Is she fertile?" Morag mocked the first question people always asked.

Sullen, I replied, "Da and Ma believe so. They say it will strengthen links with Eire."

"Politics, politics," sighed Morag wearily, sitting down on the rock beside me. "It's always about offspring and bloody alliance. Children are rare currency in this world, their value higher than a kingdom."

"Will you marry again?" I asked without thinking.

Morag didn't answer but her hand brushed her belly.

I flushed. Barely twelve months had passed since her husband and child had succumbed to the black-blood infection. "Apologies, Mog. That was tactless of me." I thought of my elder sister, Rhyn, who'd died two years past, along with her infant son. At least Morag had survived.

Reaching up, she took my hand. "Well, you are the Lord of tactless, though how else do we go forward?" A sad grin shadowed her face. "Perhaps we have no future and the church is right. Our final glory is at hand."

I grimaced, the oft-repeated phrase sharp as chalk on slate to my ears, for if fewer souls are returning to this world, they said, then surely the time had come to ascend into the next. "Yet still the Church rushes us into breeding, as though that were all that mattered."

"There's the truth of it, Mat. If you don't impregnate someone soon they'll say your bow's unstrung and you're diminished." She picked up a handful of whelks from the rock and savagely flung them one by one into the waves.

"What's the point?" I said, then tiring of this depressing talk, cast about for lighter sport. "How about you and me, Mog? I'd wager we'd produce some admirable sprats."

"Don't you sail up that cove, Mathew Pembrock. I don't want your Da getting ideas." She punched me on the leg. "Besides, I'd grind those bones of yours to pulp. You'd be dead inside a week."

My heart lifted and as I laughed the sound of church bells drifted on the wind. "Come on," I said, taking her hand and lifting her up. "Time to meet the heretic."

Dewed in sweat, we raced across the headland and dove down the narrow network of blackthorn tunnels to the harbour at New Porth Clais. Vexed, I saw the boat already moored and its red sail furled. The occupant, a thin dark haired man in dull monk's habit, already climbing a rusted ladder to where a party of officials waited.

On one side, surrounded by a cohort of ministers and guards, stood my father Lord Gruffydd, tall, barrel-chested and broad as an oak, and with him my mother, Lady Constance, a willow draped in lace. On the other side, Bishop Ellis, red-faced and fat, surrounded by his entourage of priests and novices. Everyone, except Lord Gruffydd, looked tense. My father didn't do tense. He was said to have once killed an assassin with a spoon whilst at supper, then called for fresh cutlery and dessert.

Leaving the path, we plunged into the sweltering heat of the harbour with its rank smell of rotting fish and seaweed and crossed the pitted slipway towards the unwelcoming welcome party. Flotsam laden waves lifted lazily on the falling tide while bright coloured bee-eaters soared and dipped amongst the flies.

I was soon spotted and my father's rough voice bellowed out from his great red beard, "Ah gentlemen observe. The woman who should have been a son and my son who should have been a woman."

Like trained magpies his ministers laughed on cue, while the black clad Bishop's priests maintained a sullen silence. With my face hotter than the stifling air and not trusting myself to a civil response, I set my jaw against replying.

Morag however showed no restraint. "Good day, uncle. I am afraid the humour of your remark escapes me, perhaps the summer heat has wilted it?"

"I like your fire Morag. I wish you could impart some to my son. We must find you a more robust husband to match that steel."

Morag curtsied, her smile fading.

"And as for you, my empty cannon, what's this I hear? You showed your neck to Hugh Skomer? I didn't raise you to be a coward, lad."

Sharp as flint, I replied, "The man was drunk. I don't brawl in the street with drunks."

"Then it's not because he's built like a Shire Horse and could pound you into the soil?" sneered my father. "Don't you know it's unworthy to skulk from a fight like a rat in the corn, boy? Hugh challenged our rule and that will not go unanswered. I shall have words with his father. There will be a public reckoning and I'll expect you to win."

"Oh delightful, another political farce," I muttered, knowing full well Hugh would be compelled to give me victory, a humiliation that would leave me with a fresh enemy waiting to stab me in the back one dark night. Not that Da cared. Lord Gruffydd said a man who claimed no enemies either wasn't paying attention or wasn't worth his salt.

The heretic from the boat flashed me a smile. He was travel worn but dark, sparkling eyes brightened his weathered complexion. Though a stranger, there was something oddly familiar about him that I couldn't place. His reason for being here was much the topic of whispered conversation around the bars and ale-houses of Davidseat. Was he an Electrical Evangelist, come to preach the sin of tecknowledge? All I knew was that this man had seen the world beyond the confines of our constraining shores, which stirred in me the twin sins of curiosity and jealousy.

A representative of the Bishop stepped forward and whispered something to Lord Gruffydd.

"Kazi's teeth, I've already told you," Da boomed, addressing Bishop Ellis direct. "Father Stephen will be residing at Penlan for the duration of his stay. He's under my protection for the time being, understand?"

No one dared countermand this and even Bishop Ellis restricted his protest to thin lipped disapproval.

Wrapped in troubled thoughts, I boarded one of the horse-drawn carriages. As the whip cracked and we set off towards the city of Davidseat in a cloud of dust, a frisson of unease seized me, as if I were poised above the cold churning waters of an angry sea.

Chapter 2 – The Common Clay

The following morning the sound of bells grew louder as we rattled down the tree-lined lane towards the towering spires of the cathedral. Rebuilt after the Great Tribulation it was the crowning glory of Davidseat, our family's ancient seat of power. Though small compared to the sprawling cities of ancient times it nevertheless had good roads, sound stone-built houses and had remained more or less at peace for close on a hundred years.

Passing the Bishop's palace I looked across the glebe meadow to see a stream of parishioners heading down the narrow lane from the town above. They flowed into the cathedral grounds to pool around its great ironbound doors as we pulled up.

My father and mother alighted from the carriage and headed for the crowd. I waited for Morag to join me, then revived the topic of the Skomers. "Damn Da and his love of duels. I'll fight Hugh for Pembrock honour but everyone will see it for the pantomime it is." I spat in the dust. "The Skomers planned this all along I am sure of it."

"Of course they did. Do you recall why Hugh to hit you?"

I felt my bruise. "No. We were all drinking and making merry next thing he'd walloped me."

"A clever ploy." Morag smiled at a fisherman who doffed his cap. "Being drunk he could pass off the assault as a misunderstanding, rather than an attack on your family. I expect his father put him up to it. Sir Geraint has aspirations."

"And had I brawled with him all Neo Pembrock would have seen a Skomer best Lord Gruffydd's son. The whole thing's a farce; even if I win this coming fight I lose. Can't you help, Mog? You're good with clever solutions." The mire of constant intrigue dragged at me, like seaweed in a stagnant cove.

She patted my arm. "Sorry, cousin. You're stuck in the riptide with this one. If I were you I should pray for divine intervention. I'm looking forward to Bishop Ellis's sermon."

My eyes wide, I cried in mock alarm, "I'm shocked! Has my cousin been kidnapped and replaced by an imposter? You're always telling me he's a tedious bigot."

"Oh he is," she said with demure slyness. "But I'll wager he'll inform us why your father's guest is a heretic."

Following the flock, we passed through the great doors like sheep to market and into the bosom of the church.

In the pleasant cool interior, snippets of conversation wafted around me as I made my way down the aisle between the pews.

"Old man Harris has been ill these past six weeks."

"No change then?"

"We need rain. If it don't come soon harvest will be poor."

"... ah told 'im it would turn gangrenous."

"Doc said it wouldn't 'ave lived any road, poor little mite."

"D'you hear about Davies' cows? Torn apart an' tossed around like old rags."

"Wolves?"

"A boar 'e said, but I've never seen the like."

"Molly's come down with the flux again. I've left mother looking after her."

And so it went, a litany of complaints and misfortunes, large and small.

As if seeking delivery from these burdened souls, I lifted my gaze to the three magnificent stained glass windows above the high altar. There, Jaymes Chanel the Redeemer, backed by Eastern light, gestured towards the holy city of Shambala. His consort Kazi Dayer Golden-eye, stood beside him with mismatched eyes and wolf, symbolic of her demon Rakshara past, while in the surrounding scenes the landscape transitioned from charred wasteland to fields of golden corn, symbolising the triumph of light over darkness.

Hugh was already ensconced in the Skomer pews when Morag and I reached ours. He winked at me as we took our Pembrock seats opposite.

Frowning, I nudged Morag. "What's that about? Am I to consider it an apology? Well, it won't wash my deck."

"Just ignore him," she answered.

In sour humour, I turned towards the altar. "I hate politics. When Da dies I'll abdicate. Some other fool can grasp the thorny staff."

Morag giggled, drawing a stern shush from Lord Gruffydd.

"That's what I like about you, Mat," she whispered. "Your ambition is to have no ambition. Don't make that face, it's a compliment."

Muttering quietly, I took up my book and flipped to the first hymn.

The service proceeded in the usual dull manner, but when it came to Bishop Ellis's sermon there was a palpable increase in the congregation's attention.

Leaning from the pulpit like a ponderous, fleshy gargoyle, the Bishop issued his opening remark. "From the Book of the Great Tribulation, chapter 5. *And it came to pass in the fourth year of the Great Tribulation that all the world was torn asunder. Displeased by the destruction she witnessed, Ekata stretched forth her hand and drew down her cleansing power. Ribbons of light filled the sky for seven nights and when the seventh night had passed, all things made of tecknowledge had ceased to function and a great darkness fell upon the world.*" He paused, scouring the congregation with a raptor's gaze. "Nine-hundred years or so ago, the Rainbow Storm marked the beginning of the end of that great war, which left the world scarred for one hundred years. Imagine, if you can, the terror of those people, stripped in an instant of all their power, and take comfort that this is a thing we shall never experience, for we are cleansed of the evil of tecknowledge and await our reward in the coming ascension. For is it not written? *Absolved of all sin and healed of all pain, we will stand before the Sacred Trinity; Great Ekata, Jaymes Chanel, our Lord and Risen Redeemer and Kazi Dayer, the blessed Goldeneye.*" Like a sculptor, Bishop Ellis chipped away at his argument, shaping it word by word until eventually the gist of it emerged. "I always think on these words of our Lord, Jaymes the Redeemer. *On the roof of the world there is a place for you and it is called Shambala. Those of you desiring peace come to me there. Let your troubles fall away and all your ills be healed.*" His eyes closed in rapture. "A lovely thing it must be. To experience that glorious healing touch as Jaymes rests his hand upon you." He reached out his own hand in benediction. "If only *we* had such healing power I hear you say, for it has been many long years since our city rang with the laughter of children." His eyes focused on me, Morag and the other twenty-somethings in the congregation. "Only three children, Bartrem and Lizzy Parish and Jesse Morgan, are with us today." Three invalids, more often abed than at play, I thought, as the Bishop paused momentarily to let that sink in. "Fifteen years ago a visitor came to our shores. A foreigner whom we took to our bosom, little knowing he carried with him a new strain of Blight." At this, a sullen muttering rose from the congregation. Bishop Ellis smiled. "And now we have another stranger in our midst." He stared straight at the heretic priest seated next to Lord Gruffydd. "A man who believes Shambala is not a spiritual destination but a physical place, here on Earth. Perhaps he seeks it to find a cure for the Blight and all those other ills that assail us. A worthy aim, for who would not wish an end to the terrible disease by which we are oppressed? But why stop there? Why not seek an end to failed harvests? And if that, then why not ways to shrink a day's journey to mere hours, or soar amongst the clouds in suits of iron and shape living things to our will?" He paused before delivering his final thrust. "Remember, these are the desires that led to man's downfall. Beguiling it may be to hanker after that apparent golden age but I tell you this, such desire will only lead to darkness and damnation! This is why we have the Lists of Proscription. Shambala is not of this world but of the next. And to those who would bind its divine glory in common clay I say beware, for your mouth will be filled with ash and eagles will feast upon your liver." Having delivered this arrow of verbal retribution he drew back and finished saying, "Now let us sing. Hymn 451. 'I will face the tribulations that I bear'."

There was a scraping of feet as the congregation rose. I felt a nudge and Morag leant towards me whispering, "And now we know why your father's guest is a heretic."

Chapter 3 – The First Fall of the Axe

Why would my father incur the wrath of the church by entertaining such a dangerous heretic? It made no sense, but confronting Lord Gruffydd was ever a futile task, so later that afternoon I sought out my mother.

I found Lady Constance in the castle orchard with a servant, tending her fruit trees. Insects hummed in the dappled shade and the daisy-speckled grass still held that early luscious green, before midsummer baked it brown.

"Good afternoon Ma. How are the pears progressing?"

Lifting the broad brim of her old straw hat, Lady Constance's watery blue-eyes regarded me warmly. "Mathew, dear boy. How delightful. I had a feeling you might call by. The pears are doing nicely, thank you for asking, though I fear our medlar is afflicted with rot and will have to be grubbed out if infection is not to spread."

"I see no medlars in the garden, Ma," I said with a crafty smile.

Lifting a delicate hand to examine a faded leaf Lady Constance replied innocently, "Really? I could swear one came into the castle yesterday." She wafted across to another tree to check for pests. "Your father is an enthusiastic but poor gardener. He acquires new plants without considering their suitability and sometimes doesn't know if he's pulling up roses or planting weeds."

I grinned, just like her sun-bleached hair tied tight beneath her hat, mother kept her machinations hidden. "Do you always talk in metaphors Ma?"

"When everything in life is a metaphor, it's hard not to." She snipped off a brown-edged leaf. "Come, embrace your mother properly, then we'll chat." She placed the pruners in the open wicker basket on her arm and turned to me with her other arm held wide.

Gingerly I wrapped my arms about her delicate frame and kissed the proffered cheek. Her soft downy skin yielded to my lips and the aromas of lavender and fresh hay stood in stark contrast to my father, whose personal scent carried the smell of horses, dogs and alcohol.

Taking me by the arm, Lady Constance led us over to the summerhouse.

"Chamomile tea and biscuits," she said and a sharp click of her delicate white fingers sent the servant scurrying to the kitchen. "I hear you have a fight coming up."

I sighed. "And don't I wish I could avoid it. Da thinks it will restore my honour but I'm very much afraid it will have the opposite effect."

"Tsk. Typical. Your father used to be so much better at diplomacy. Now he clings to his position like a bad-tempered bear. He hoards enemies like a miser and squanders friends like a gambler and it has left him destitute of good men."

"At least I have Morag. If I could find a wife with her spark I'd consider myself well blessed. She's a good friend and suits my temper well."

Mother gave me a weak smile. "That's nice. It's sweet that you think well of my niece."

The servant returned with a pot of chamomile tea and a plate of biscuits plus two antique china cups and saucers.

I studied the faded yellow tray on which the items sat. "Where did this come from?"

"A dig at Caerfyrddin. They often salvage interesting artefacts."

Wondering if Coca-Cola was the name of the smiling woman depicted or the artist who created it, I said, "I thought the church didn't approve? Is it not on the Lists of Proscription?"

"Oh they don't mind a little digging. It's the exhuming of ancient knowledge they view with a dim light."

I selected a biscuit. "Then why is that heretic priest here at Da's pleasure instead of being handed over to the church examiners?"

"Ah, so now we get to the nub of it." Lady Constance smiled and put down her cup. "You think your father prays to saints but courts devils?"

"Doesn't he?"

"You could ask him?"

"If it were that easy I wouldn't be here... Sorry," I said, seeing her brow furrow. "You know I love your company. Aside from Mog you're the only one who understands me."

Her demeanour blossomed once more. "I know, dear. Now listen, our guest has an audience with your father later this evening. The library next door will be locked, but I will be returning a book around seven, if you need to find me."

"Thank you, Ma," I said.

Lady Constance placed a thin hand on my rough fist. "You are the best of us Mathew, but you need to learn to use those wits I gave you. Do not let yourself be strangled by politics."

"I won't, Ma," I replied, though I felt the tendrils of schemes and intrigue creep over me.

"And don't be afraid to push back against your father."

"I try but it isn't easy."

With eyes that suddenly seemed tired she looked at me strangely and said, "Walk with me, Mathew."

Guiding me by the arm she led me to an old apple tree on the far side of the orchard. Its canopy was thin and dead branches stood out stark against the sun, while its hollow trunk gaped like the maw of a rotten corpse.

"This old tree has long been a favourite of mine. It is sad to see it in such a poor state." Lady Constance reached out and touched the cankered bark as if it were a lover. "When I was a child my father gave it to the previous Lord Pembrock as an assurance. He said if the tree survived then when I came of age, I would wed Lord Pembrock's son. The tree thrived and so I married your father. It's over forty years old now and I have loved it all that time, but now it is diseased and bears little fruit. I could let it carry on for the sake of sentiment, but the disease may spread to other trees and I am too practical for such matters. Sometimes you have to let go of something you cherish to preserve the rest of what you love." She whistled a shrill note to a man trimming cordons by the garden wall. When he looked up she pointed to the tree and made a swift chopping motion with her hand.

As the man went to his barrow of tools she said, "It will not serve you well to fight Hugh Skomer. Avoid it if you can."

"If I do, all Pembrock will think me a coward."

"There are better ways to display bravery than wielding a sword, dear boy. I'm sure you'll find one. Now, don't forget I'll be at the library at seven," and with that she kissed my cheek, just as the first axe blow shattered the peace.

Chapter 4 – Hope and Hidden Purpose

Later, as I climbed the back stairs, I pondered on my mother's words. She was right, of course, I shouldn't let father rule me, but standing up to Lord Gruffydd was no easy matter. If I was going to turn him from persisting in the ridiculous notion of my fighting Hugh Skomer, I could do with some leverage.

Shadows lengthening with the approach of evening, I entered the long corridor, its pale painted walls exuding heat absorbed throughout the day. Passing by a narrow window, I paused. Far to the east, in a veil of blue haze, the broken remnants of the Great Demonline wall were just visible, like a row of inland sea stacks. They brought to mind legendary tales and dreams of strange creatures, eliciting a dark thrill and a yearning to know more of the world beyond Neo Pembrock. Idly I wondered which parent had gifted me this streak of restlessness.

The sound of the cathedral bells ringing the hour roused me from my reverie and I hurried on to find Lady Constance waiting outside the library.

She smiled in that quiet way that hid her inner steel. "Good, you came alone. I hoped you would. No need to tell Morag everything."

"She's not my shadow, Ma," I said.

"I should hope not. Now here is the spare key to the library. I will lock up as I go but expect a servant to check in sometime. Your father wants nothing untoward to disturb this meeting."

"Thanks again, Ma. Do you wish me to tell you what went on?"

"Bless you, dear boy, but it is not necessary." Mother put a delicate hand to my cheek. "Now, no more talk. I am expected in the hall. Just remember to use that brain of yours. It could do with the exercise."

I entered the room and Lady Constance locked the door behind me. I stood a while in the stillness, listening to the fading swish of her dress as she moved away down the corridor. When she had passed out of hearing I removed my heavy clumping boots and positioned a leather chair with its winged-back to the door. Finally I made a short tour of the library, running my hand over the dark shelves of musty books. Faint scuff marks on the floor and a weak draft of air from a bookcase betrayed the hidden access to father's study. I listened at the slim gap but all I could hear was the regular tick of his longcase clock.

Taking down a cloth-bound volume of Pascal's 'Tales from the Scriptures", I skipped to a favoured story in the book and settled down in the chair to wait. It was the one where Jaymes Chanel battles Kazi Dayer in her demon Rakshara form. After a long and violent fight, the divine Jaymes won but instead of killing Kazi he chose to be merciful and by the power of his divine touch, healed the demon of her wounds. Converted by this act of love, Kazi renounced her flesh-eating ways and swore eternal allegiance to Ekata. Henceforth she was ever at Jaymes's side in his fight against evil. In my mind I imagined myself bestowing such mercy on Hugh, to gasps from an appreciative crowd. *If only life were that simple*, I sighed.

A muffled slam evicted me from my dreaming and I heard the lusty laugher of Lord Gruffydd pass unimpeded through the wall like water through a sieve.

Quietly, I pressed my ear to the gap of the hidden door to listen.

"How are you feeling after that ecumenical thrust from the Bishop earlier?" came my father's rugged voice.

"I am used to such blows Gruff, I can roll with them," answered a softer educated voice I had to strain to hear. The informal familiarity came as a surprise; people were usually more deferential around my father.

Lord Gruffydd gave a brief laugh. "Well step carefully, *Father* Stephen," he said, laying heavy emphasis on the word father. "The Bishop can deliver more than verbal blows should he choose to do so. The sooner you are away the better."

"Amen to that," said Father Stephen, "though I don't understand. I thought the Bishop was amenable to my quest?"

"He is, in some small measure."

"Then he has a curious way of showing it."

"The Bishop preaches ascension to keep the masses subdued but behind all that pomp he's as worried as the rest of us. Don't let that defuse your vigilance however. The tenets of the faith always come first. He sticks to the Lists of Proscription and will not tolerate unbridled heresy."

"And what of you, Gruff?" asked Father Stephen, with astonishing directness.

Lord Gruffydd replied coldly. "I am a true believer Stephen. You know that."

"And yet I am here in your study and not in your dungeon being tortured or awaiting burning."

Lord Gruffydd huffed. "I'm no heretic, as you well know, but I've a pragmatic turn of mind. I do what's needed to protect my people and if that takes me to the margins of sin then add it to my deathbed confessions. In the meantime, we need a solution to end this Blight that withers us."

"I take it that your doctors can't help?"

My father gave a cynical snort. "Glorified faith healers appointed by the church. They have some knowledge of hygiene at least but little else and they cannot fill a barren womb. Not even with their own pricks, though I hear some try. Let me come to the point, Stephen. In your letter, you spoke of a place where ancient knowledge may yet be preserved."

"Llys Tywyll. It was the seat of the Rakshara Shadow Court in pre-chaos times. I believe it to be little more than a week's ride from here."

"Former seat I hope." Lord Gruffydd said, "I can do without demons coming a-knocking on my door."

"Have no fear. All the Rakshara are long gone. Your people would be dead or slaves by now if this were not the case."

"Humph! I suppose. However, there are many rumoured repositories of ancient wisdom and all are cursed ruins with nothing but death to welcome the curious. Why should this Llys Tywyll be any different?"

"There are no tales of it ever being ransacked."

Lord Gruffydd snorted. "There may be good reason for that. Have you not considered the danger?"

"I believe the risks are manageable and the prize worth it." I heard the sound of rummaging. "Here! One of the potential treasures we might recover."

"What's this? A manuscript?"

"An ancient text, bound onto cloth to preserve it. On loan, shall we say, from the archives of my order in Truro."

There came the sound of something being unrolled and Lord Gruffydd said, "What in Ekata's name is *IVF?*"

"An ancient medical practice to increase fertility, or so I understand. The leaflet you see was produced to give an overview of the process. I believe it was given to patients awaiting treatment."

A curious excitement entered my father's voice. "So you're telling me the pre-Tribulation people had fertility problems too, but found a solution?"

"Precisely," said Father Stephen.

I felt my father's great exhale of breath as if it were my own. "If true, this answers all our prayers but are you sure this mythical Court holds such knowledge?"

"Documents in Truro indicate the Shadow Court held a vast library of ancient texts, both demon and human. I would say the prospects are good, if it still survives."

A brief silence followed, then Lord Gruffydd's voice came, "A flimsy hope but I suppose the rewards are too great to ignore." He took on a more practical tone. "What of beast Rakshara? The demons may be gone but their bastard offspring still inhabit the Forbidden Lands."

"I agree, the devolved dregs of demonkind are a significant potential danger but I am not unprepared. You know me Gruff. I don't go paddling a leaking boat without a sail."

"True. You have survived this long I suppose. Very well. I can give you Captain Beech and two good men for security. As you know, we excavate the past for resources, providing nothing recovered contravenes the List. I'm sure I can persuade the Bishop to treat this as such a mission. However the church will insist on having their own man on board, to weed out anything *blasphemous* you might uncover."

"That could prove awkward." Father Stephen's tone faltered.

"Oh, I'm sure seeking medical knowledge will pass muster, unless there is another side to this you are not telling me Stephen."

There followed a gap, then Father Stephen said, "I hope to find clues to the location of Shambala."

To my surprise father chuckled at this blasphemy. "Oh Stephen you never change. Well, it's not my task to tell you how to waste your life but you'd better keep that agenda hidden or things might get a little too warm for you understand?"

"Oh don't worry. I have no intention of being roasted. Now if we've nothing else to discuss I will take my leave. I wouldn't like it to get about that you were consorting with heretics."

"Surely you cannot pass up a little nightcap? It has been many years since last we talked."

I pressed my eager ear to the secret door. What was this relationship the two of them had? They spoke as if they were old friends or acquaintances.

"Well maybe just the one. Perhaps a toast to our mutual father? What say you, brother?" replied Father Stephen in a calculating voice.

Brother! The word struck me like a crack to the head, exploding my world. In all my life I'd never known or imagined that my father had a brother!

Chapter 5 – The Gulf Between Them

A thick mist rolled in off the sea filling the deep lanes with fog, leaving Penlan Castle an island in a sea of cloud.

"Just the weather for sloping off with a heretic." Morag shivered and folded her arms against the morning chill.

Pulling up the collar of my new black cassock to ward off the damp air, I replied haughtily, "I'm not sloping. I'm a Church official. An Examiner no less, with papers granting Father Stephen temporary passage, signed and sealed by Bishop Ellis himself. Providing, of course the heretic doesn't try to preach any vile heretical nonsense."

Morag punched me lightly on the arm. "Don't be pompous, Mat. I know you don't really want to be an Examiner. You're only doing this to get out of fighting Hugh."

"So? It got me a free pass from Bishop Ellis to escape this pit of intrigue."

She glanced to the east where the sun's yellow disc peeked over the horizon. "Well you'll roast in that coat before long, besides putting the fear of roasting into those you meet."

"I'm not roasting anyone Morag, and I don't believe the slurs they tell about the Examiners."

Morag laughed. "Oh don't get all pious with me. You were only moaning about them the other day."

"I'm just upholding the faith," I sniffed, with more than a little air of self-importance.

Morag gave me a condescending pat on the shoulder. "Of course you are! Come on. Tell the truth now. I want to know how you managed to wheedle your way onto this little venture."

My lips remained sealed, except for lifting at the corners to form a smug curve. Bishop Ellis had been only too happy to snub Da by appointing me.

"Keep your secrets then," Morag said feigning disinterest. "But you're only doing this because you're desperate for adventure."

"This isn't a pleasure trip," I replied, barely stifling my eagerness. Life had been so dull since mother had father pull me from the militia.

"Of course not," said Morag. "Any-a-way you take care and try not to trip over your new calling."

"I will," I said with a warm smile.

She's putting on weight, I thought as she sidled away. Much more castle food and I'll be the same.

Lady Constance approached, kissed me lightly on the cheek and pressed a small object into the palm of my hand. "A talisman to keep you safe."

I looked down at the silver wolf's head ring; it had one eye of green emerald and one of golden amber. "I can't take this, Ma, it's priceless."

"You are priceless, dear boy, and I want you safe. The Goldeneye has protected our family from demons for countless generations. Take it and may it keep their eyes off you."

Sliding the ring onto the third finger of my right hand, I thanked her adding, "I'll return it, don't you worry."

"See that you do." She gripped my cassock coat, her hand ghostly against the dark wool. "This black doesn't suit you. It may take you away from the fight," she glanced briefly at Lord Gruffydd, "but it will attract sharks. Don't cling to it longer than you have to."

"It's only an honorary position, Ma. To become a proper Church Examiner takes years of training, but I need to look authoritative."

A curious sadness came into mother's eyes. "I am planning a trip to Eire, to see family. I may not be here on your return but you are welcome to join me there should you wish."

Something in the way she said it struck me. "Is Da not accompanying you?"

"No. He's off hunting some huge boar spotted over in Mynydd forest and you know how your father likes a challenge."

"At least it will sate his bloodlust. Enjoy your trip, Ma. I'll be back before you know it."

Saying nothing she drew me to her, and held me with a greedy desperation that was embarrassing and comforting in equal measure.

Still, this melancholy parting was not enough to clip the wings of my soaring spirit. Finally, I was going beyond the kingdom and my childhood dreams of travel and adventure were becoming real.

I checked the saddle on my horse and the items I'd packed; bedding roll, food, water, waxed cloak, spare clothing, fire making kit and a large purse of money, another parting gift from mother. Of weapons I'd selected my pearl-handled dagger of Damascus steel, a customised carriage bow with quiver of hunting arrows and an elegant short sword engraved with a welsh dragon and silver inlay on the guard. I hoped that would suffice.

Lord Gruffydd snuck up behind me. "So His Grace put you with the Cigfrân did he, lad? Seems then you won't be fighting young Skomer after all."

My face hardened. Cigfrân, or Flesh Crow, was rude slang for a Church Examiner. "It must be disappointing for you, not to have the opportunity to watch your son embarrass himself."

"I would not have taken pleasure from it. All the same, it was not wise to let the insult rest. The Skomers put us in a weak light and a fight seemed the best way to restore honour but then you went and scuppered that, didn't you?" He fixed me with narrow eyes.

"I used my initiative to gain advantage. You taught me a man needs advantage in this life."

"I taught you to fight, not skulk in shadows like a low assassin. Listening into private conversations and blackmailing your father. It's not my way," implying it was mother's.

Holding his gaze I whispered, "Say what you like. The Bishop trusts me but I am not his puppet. This way keeps your brother safe and protects our family honour."

"I agree."

"I… beg pardon?" Father's admission threw me.

Attending to the horse, Lord Gruffydd sighed. "You found a more elegant solution and delivered it with admirable cunning. I am sure Constance had a hand in that but nevertheless it was well done."

Praise from father was so rare I was struck speechless.

Lord Gruffydd however, raced on, gruff, ill-practiced words tumbling from him in an awkward cascade. "We've never really got on, you and I, that can't be helped now, but… I mean to say… You are not the son I would have wished for but I don't hate you… So! There it is!"

Father cuffed me roughly across the arm in lieu of an embrace, pushing against the barrier that held his affection in check. In that moment I saw the limits of my father's strength and the gulf between us, too wide to cross.

Mounting my horse, I proffered a smile, which my father returned with the briefest nod of taciturn approval. Then, Captain Beech called and it was time to leave.

The Captain was weathered and solid, like a sea lashed mooring post. I had served under him when in the militia. Jon Beech, they said, could gut a man as easily as a fish and still show respect for both.

"*Master* Pembrock. Glad you could join us," he said as I drew alongside.

This was no reference to my youth. Master was the standard term of address for an Examiner and yet the Captain made it sound like a bad taste in the mouth.

Jon Beech wheeled his horse around to face the small group of mounted men. "Right, gentlemen. For those who weren't privy to our earlier discussion, that's you Mr Pryce," he nodded to Edwin Pryce, a thickset muscular young man, who had trained alongside me, "and Mr L'Ombre." Jacques L'Ombre, a thin man, with piercing grey eyes and sharp features, sat impassive in his saddle. "First, we are travelling to Caerfyrddin. After that, Father Stephen here will outline where fortune takes us next." He indicated the heretic priest who sat easily on his horse as if it were second nature. "As you can see, the Church also has an interest in our mission." He indicated me. "Our purpose is not to be discussed or speculated on until we reach Caerfyrddin. Is that clear?" Pryce, L'Ombre and I nodded, while Father Stephen merely shrugged. "Good. Let's get underway."

Turning our horses to the road, a flock of black crows left the castle walls and flew over our heads. With harsh laughing cries they swooped low over the fields and disappeared into the mist.

Chapter 6 – A Village of Ghosts

By the time we hit the coast road, other travellers were abroad; locals on foot, hawkers with handcarts and wagons laden with all manner of goods rattled along the dusty track. Caerfyrddin was nearly thirty miles distant, but the slow traffic meant an hour and a half later we still hadn't reached the river ferry at Solvamouth.

"Too many abandoned houses," commented Father Stephen on passing yet another boarded up property.

"No heir to inherit," I said.

An old couple leading a donkey stopped to watch us pass, their faces hardening into sour frowns as they saw me. I got much the same response from other travellers and it didn't take long to realise that my presence on the road was about as welcome as a bailiff at a wedding party. Only Captain Jon Beech, two score years and five with hair receding didn't treat me as a potential inquisitor. Eddie, with whom I had spent many a drunken night, ignored me completely and Jacques L'Ombre, shot me sullen scowls whenever I glanced in his direction. All I knew of him was he was French and that behind his back the men-at-arms called him "Jack the Rat". Personally I thought he rather resembled a fox. Father Stephen thankfully kept his opinions to himself.

Leaving the coast road and its heavy traffic behind at Pencwm our party turned inland. It saddened me to see so many of Neo Pembrock's rolling fields returning to scrub and farms lying derelict through lack of hands to work them. Even so, there were still places where industry still thrived. In dappled woods the charcoal burners continued to charge the air with stinging smoke and some fields still shone fresh with new green crops.

Always before us was the ragged line of the Great Demonline wall, growing closer with each passing mile, a giant jawline of broken teeth, shimmering in the summer heat, I contemplated the immensity of its ruined presence, imagining it as a metaphor for my life. The barriers I'd grown up with were breaking down and through the crumbling gaps I thought I could glimpse freedom.

The morning ride continued without incident and we made good time, though the fields became more unkempt and overgrown as we neared the village of Llanglwellyn around midday, a mournful place where former homes stood forlorn and vacant with grime-encrusted windows.

"By Jay not another ghost village," said Edwin.

"Ghost village?" The term was new to me.

Edwin answered, "They've become common since you last patrolled. Not enough people. Villages are falling empty all across the land."

In amongst the silent houses I saw other, longer abandoned dwellings slowly being reclaimed by nature, roofs weighed down by age and ivy collapsing into mossy hollows where trees pushed through what had once been living space. I thought of the three children the Bishop had mentioned in his sermon back at Davidseat. What a desolate world they would inherit, if they survived to adulthood.

"Not entirely empty I hope," said Captain Beech. "I have an old friend who lives near the inn. If we break our journey there I'll take a drink with him."

Shortly we came to the old inn. It was closed, though captain Beech noted that someone had at least taken the trouble to board up the windows.

He squinted through the shutters beneath the sadly creaking weathered sign, and said, "Well, lads, there you have it. The Pen-y-Baedd is no more. Alas no drinks for us. Where's the justice in that for thirsty men?" Swinging gently in the hot air, the faded sign offered no answer. "Ten years past, this place was alive with the crack of good conversation and now... nothing."

"Captain Beech, Captain Beech, I've found something." Edwin's blonde head appeared from around the corner of the inn where he had gone exploring. "Over here!"

We hurried round to see what he'd discovered.

"Hope it's a barrel of ale, I could do with a drink," quipped Jacques.

Instead, we found a goat. Tethered to a long chain it occupied a well cropped circle of grass along the edge of a stream. Around it were the rotting tables and benches of the inn's garden.

"Well it appears someone still lives here," said Father Stephen.

Ignoring him, Captain Beech headed past the goat to a low wooden gate set into a neatly trimmed hedge and called out, "Alain! Alain are you there?"

No answer came back but as we entered the tidy sunlit garden we were met by the sound of angry buzzing.

"Bees!" said Edwin, seeing three brightly painted hives. "Bees mean honey!"

"Alain!" called out Captain Beech again.

The garden appeared well tended, as if the owner had just popped out for a moment, except closer inspection showed a haze of weed seedlings on the tilled soil and unpicked summer fruiting raspberries rotting on the bushes.

Jacques pointed to a walking stick lying abandoned by some steps. "Is that your friend's?"

"It wasn't when I saw him a year ago," said Captain Beech heading past the stick towards the house, calling as he went.

Neither Edwin nor I knew the man who lived there but we both shared in the Captain's growing concern.

The white-washed cottage was a pretty sight, dazzling in the midday sun, with a low slate roof and a joyous cascade of rambling pink roses framing its open door. As the sound of bees faded behind us, a second, less welcome droning of flies came from the open door, accompanied by a smell that was not honey or roses.

"Merde," whispered Jacques.

"Not shit, monsieur," Father Stephen intoned solemnly. "Death."

The Captain went inside while I and the others waited in silence.

After a while he re-emerged, pale as bleached stone. "Alain's dead. Been gone a week I reckon. Looks like a fall. Broken leg or hip. He's down by the kitchen table. I wouldn't go in if I were you."

"So what happens now?" asked Jacques in a brusque manner that touched the border of callousness.

The Captain peered at the high sun as if drawing strength from its heat. Eventually he said, "Dig a hole, where those cabbages are looks easiest. I expect you'll find tools in the shed. I'll see to the body. Father Stephen, might I ask you to perform the service when all is prepared?"

Father Stephen nodded.

Captain Beech returned to the cottage, while we collected tools and set to work digging the grave. As the Captain had surmised, the ground was soft and easy to work. A short while later he returned and took over some of the digging until a reasonable hole was excavated.

"It's not that deep," I said, wiping a dirty hand across my forehead.

Jacques lent heavily on the spade he'd been using, "Well, it'll have to do. Dig further and the sides might collapse. Besides, je suis crevé."

Edwin's brow creased. "Crevay?"

"Knackered. Done in," Jacques explained.

The digging done, Captain Beech carried the body from the house, wrapped in a white sheet. I had to hold my breath against the stench of rotting flesh as the bundle was lowered into the hole.

In light of the smell and in contrast to normal procedure, we voted to fill in the grave before Father Stephen commenced his brief service.

"Ashes to ashes, dust to dust and may the gates of Sambhala open to his soul," he intoned with solemn dignity.

"Shouldn't we cover the mound?" I asked. "Stones or something, to stop foxes or other animals digging."

Captain Beech looked about the garden. "Not much to use around here and the sun is already way past noon. We'll let it be. Alain liked foxes, he used to feed them. If it happens that he does so again, well I don't think he would mind."

"Is this what's coming for all of us?" I stared at the dark mound of soil. "Dying alone, with no one to help, if we don't find a cure for the Blight."

"Aye," said Captain Beech. "That's the broad fit of it."

"Except there'll be no one to bury you," added Jacques with dark humour.

Before leaving the village to its ghosts, we released the goat. There was no debate about this, even though it was a valuable food source. No one, aside from Jacques, felt like eating and we'd all had enough death for one day.

While Father Stephen and Jacques checked the saddles on their horses, I went back to get the Captain and Edwin who had remained in the garden. As I reached the gate I saw them with their backs turned standing by the graveside. They hadn't seen me and it seemed wrong to interrupt such a private moment so I hung back.

Over the soporific buzzing of the bees I heard Edwin say, "You okay Jon?"

"It is what it is, Eddie. These things happen," answered the captain ever the stoic.

They stood apart yet seemed linked by an invisible bond.

"Don't worry. I'll take care of you… when the time comes." Edwin's hand lifted towards the captain's.

Captain Beech turned away from it, yet couldn't quite suppress the emotion in his reply, "But who will look after you, Eddie? Who will look after you?"

Chapter 7 – The Carrion Crow

The brightly painted houses of Caerfyrddin clustered around the remains of the Demonline like crumbs around a ruined cake. Knowing my ancestors had built that colossal structure stirred in me a deep sense of family pride. However that pride became muted as we climbed the steep, rambling streets in late afternoon. My Examiner vestments drew unfriendly stares from the people we passed, while the heretic, Father Stephen, barely garnered a curious glance.

The streets led us to a square with a central metal pole. Blackened manacles hung from it and a large circle of pale grey ash spread out from its base. The fire that had cracked the cobbles was long dead but the horror and anger of it still smouldered in the faces of the townsfolk. A soft breeze stirred the flakes, causing them to rise up like ghosts and as the horror sank into me I began to seriously question my choice of office. The people looked upon me as if my own murderous hand had lit the pyre.

Bowed in silence our group reached the Gatehouse Inn. Built of rough grey stone it appeared to be either emerging from, or swallowed by, the town's main section of Demonline, soaring above it like a great sea cliff. Huge blocks of wall had tumbled down to hug the surrounding houses in a stone embrace of inland coves; such that I half expected the tide to come rushing down the streets.

"Unusual hostelry." Father Stephen scanned the narrow slit windows and crenellations on the Gatehouse tower.

Captain Beech's reply was plain and factual. "It was a former keep when the demon threat was real. It's been an inn now for two centuries or more."

"Still, the Great Demonline is impressive, even in this dilapidated state." Father Stephen craned his head back to take in the full height of the wall.

Not wishing to be left out, I imparted a slice of my own family knowledge. "David the First of Neo Pembrock built it after he drove back the Rakshara and brought peace to these lands. They say it took two thousand men twenty-five years to construct."

"Hmm," said Father Stephen.

"You don't believe me?"

"The last true Rakshara were defeated at the Battle of El Chorro in 2062."

Perceiving this a slur on my family, I replied sharply. "Perhaps, perhaps not, but an ancestor, on my mother's side, General Daniel Carrington, was in command of the battle you speak of. He vanquished an army of Rakshara led by the Spider-queen, Ariadnii, herself."

"Wasn't *Colonel* Carrington killed?" Father Stephen said, casually correcting my claim.

Beginning to dislike this priest, heretic, uncle or whatever, I replied acidly, "You mean lost. He disappeared whilst in pursuit of a retreating band of demons. His actual fate remains unknown."

Before the debate could escalate, Captain Beech cut in. "Finish the history lesson later. Right now I want our horses stabled so we can sort out rooms. Then, Master Pembrock, you can meet me on the cast of the Demonline for battle practice."

"Battle practice?" I said. "What for?"

"We head for the Forbidden Lands tomorrow. I'd hate to go in unprepared. Bring whichever weapon you feel you need most practice with." Captain Beech led his horse off to the stables, calling back over his shoulder, "half an hour."

Father Stephen bowed lightly and smiled. "Well I won't keep you from your swordplay, Master Pembrock. Don't take offence. The Great Demonline really is a magnificent achievement, given the trying times your ancestor lived in."

Soured by this veiled taunt, I watched the priest depart with a growing loathing, but then decided that as a representative of the Church, even a temporary one, I should rise above such personal feelings, so, after stabling my horse and dumping my travel pack, I wandered off to find a church. It would be expected of an Examiner and it seemed more important to play the part I'd adopted than running around a field wielding steel.

I'd visited Caerfyrddin several years previously with the militia and knew well the little church down near the river. The mistrustful glowers my Examiner vestments received en route reminded me of the ashes in the square. Briefly, I considered going back to change but it was the clothes they hated not me. I could bear that for the sake of the mission.

Passing a corner pub, with dull windows and green streaks staining its lime-washed walls, a group of drunken men with baleful glances raised their voices in doleful song.

A carrion crow sat on an oak
Watching the world from under his cloak
Sing heigh ho the carrion crow
Where does your sharp eye go?

The carrion crow began to rave
And called a poor farmer a crooked knave
Sing heigh ho the carrion crow
Where does your sharp lie go?

I hurried on but their voices followed me.

The carrion crow cried Ekata above
And put his hand in his fine black glove
Sing heigh ho the carrion crow
Where does your sharp knife go?

Once I'd enjoyed such drinking songs, but the bar room ballad sounded chilling now the song was directed at me.

With the venomous lyrics still haunting me, I came to the church, red sandstone, with a steep slate roof and a narrow graveyard that extended along the valley. The sound of the breeze rustling through the trees and the gentle flow of the river imbued the setting with a meditative calm. My heart easing, I absorbed the happier song of birds flitting in the leafy branches as I approached the entrance to the church.

The weather-worn doors complained loudly as I pushed them open, disturbing the quiet sanctity within. Dark wood pews contrasted sharply with bare, white walls and the only extravagance on show, a fabulously detailed stained glass window lit up the interior with subtle colour. I gazed at the raised lectern, carved in the form of a black crow with outstretched wings. It represented Cutcaw, the Straddler of Worlds, who meted out judgement in the name of Ekata. Comforted that being called a crow wasn't necessarily a bad thing I took a seat and closed my eyes in prayer.

Wrapped in the blanketing quiet, suffused with the aromas of dusty wood and a delicate memory of incense I let my mind drift. The church door opened and fell back with a bang that echoed around the walls shattering the silence. Then came the sharp click of nailed boots on stone and three male voices began to sing in an off key slur.

The poor old farmer confessed his sin
And the carrion crow began to grin
Heigh ho sang the carrion crow
Into the fire you go

I spun round. The men from the pub advanced towards me slapping heavy wooden clubs in time to the song. Regretting now that I'd left my dagger back at the inn, I balled my hands into fists in readiness to defend myself.

With a clack, the church door opened a second time and a voice I recognised called out. "That hardly seems an appropriate song for church. What say you Mr Pryce?" Captain Beech strode leisurely down the aisle with his hand resting lightly on the hilt of his sword.

Following him, Edwin Pryce replied, "Sounds like blasphemy to me Captain." He too carried a sword.

"And what about you, Monsieur L'Ombre?" asked Captain Beech.

Twirling a long, well used dagger, Jacques L'Ombre replied in a rough French drawl, "I would call it justified criticism of a corrupt regime."

"There you have it, lads," said Captain Beech putting himself between the three rapidly sobering men and me, while Edwin and Jacques stood close by. "A difference of opinion. Now, how do you suppose we resolve this within the broad embrace of a civilised society?"

Looking more nervous than belligerent, the drunks didn't answer; paying close attention, no doubt, to the swords and the odds, which had now swung away from them.

In the absence of a reply, Captain Beech ventured a solution. "Well there's lively debate or good honest duelling." The way he said it suggested he was happy with either.

The men from the pub hesitated then let their clubs drop to their sides.

Captain Beech smiled but not in a friendly way. "I'll tell you what lads. Why don't you go back to your drinking and discuss which method you prefer, while we go do our weapons practice. Then if you decide you want to take this fascinating debate further, you can come find us."

"Maybe we will," said the lead man, though his compatriot's downcast eyes suggested they would rather let the matter lie.

With slow movement Captain Beech lifted his sword a fraction from its scabbard and took a step forward. "Then we'll be sure to make you welcome."

"Come on leave it, Gren. T'aint worth it," said one of the other drunks.

Pulled by his friends, the man Gren turned away reluctantly but as he and his fellows made their way back along the aisle he turned back and shouted, "One of them his Cigfrân kind burned in the square were my brother. He weren't no heretic."

"Gren leave it." One of the others took Gren by the arm but he shook him off.

"He harmed no one, d'you hear me. No one."

"Gren!"

"But them as did it paid for it all right and you'll pay too. You mark my words."

"For fuck's sake, Gren come on."

The other two men grabbed Gren by the arms and hurried him out of the door like rats before a chambermaid's broom.

With the drunks gone, Captain Beech turned to me. "Now! I believe *Master* Pembrock, your presence is required on the training ground. So if you would care to join us we'll escort you safely back to the inn where you may select your weapon of choice." Then he added almost casual. "Might I enquire, do you have a change of attire?"

"I have my old militia uniform. I thought it more practical for the Forb... for where we are going," I said, sounding less a Church official and more like an errant pupil.

A barely suppressed sharpness entered the Captain's voice. "Excellent! So for Ekata's sake do us all a bloody favour and lose that odious black costume or else paint a target on your back. We're not in Davidseat now."

He strode off leaving me gawping after him like a stunned fish. Captain Beech had never spoken so harshly to me.

"Why did you have to go and join the Cigfrân Mat?" muttered Edwin, following the Captain's outburst.

"It's just an honorary position," I pleaded. "Bishop Ellis said I needed to show authority."

Jacques gave a sneer. "Screw the Bishop. There's no honour in the Cigfrân out here. Their authority cuts little support, as you've just seen."

"Then why are you here?" I said, embarrassed and defensive.

Jacques replied, "We go where we're ordered. Why are you here?"

"To keep an eye on the heretic," I replied, not wishing to divulge my own complex reasons, which I barely understood myself.

The Frenchman's laugh echoed through the church. "They don't care about the heretic, you connard. It's only the fucking Bishop they hate."

Chapter 8 – Taking the Bait

Step by laborious step and clutching a flask of Gatehouse ale, I wound my way up the stone stairwell, worn smooth by countless generations. Eventually I reached the top of the Demonline and breathed heavily as a warm breeze caressed my face. I stood a moment, mulling over the day's events in my mind and watching the evening swifts scream as they dived and swooped through a sky of darkening blue. I'd abandoned the black Examiner vestments for the dull green of my old militia cloak and tunic but the taint of the Cigfrân still clung. The fire-blackened poles in the town square far below still haunted me. No one had been burned in Davidseat for as long as I could remember. It was something one only joked about and the true horror of what it meant made no impression on me until now. I hadn't seen any other Examiners around town, whether because they had moved on or because, as Gren had suggested, the town folk had dealt with them. It didn't seem prudent to ask.

The sound of laughter and conversation drifted up on the warm evening air. I looked down to the

Gatehouse below where I'd seen Captain Beech and the others relaxing. Not Father Stephen though, I hadn't seen him since before practice and hoped my rebellious uncle wasn't lying dead in some back ally. In truth though, it didn't seem likely. No one in Caerfyrddin seemed much to care about his heretical beliefs. The Church alone seemed to be the focus of their anger.

In the light of the dipping sun I looked about for a place to sit. The wall was broad, about twenty-one paces wide, and its baked surface radiated heat. Lengthwise, it ran the length of the town and a good three fields beyond before ending in a shattered cliff of masonry. On the East side, it presented a smooth, lichen-encrusted barrier of ancient concrete, which had crumbled in places, leaving exposed stone blocks for plants to colonise. Cautiously, I crossed a narrow section where part of the wall had tumbled away, the debris forming a rough pyramid of rubble and boulders that splayed out over the Eastern fields. It seemed deserted but by the light of the setting sun I saw a second figure in the lea of an old guard shelter.

The figure looked up and waved. "Ah, Master Pembrock. Have you come to marvel at the skills of your ancestors or to admire the view?"

"Both... *Uncle*," I replied, after checking we were alone.

Savouring the look of surprise on the man's face, I picked my way over and, sitting down next to him, offered my flask of ale as a gesture of good faith.

Accepting it with quiet caution, Father Stephen took a calculated sip and then said, "Why do you call me *uncle*?"

"I overheard your conversation with Da."

"Ah!" He took another measure of ale before passing the flask back to me.

The eyes of the heretic priest, I noted, were the same dark shade as my father's. "So are you Da's brother? He never mentioned any siblings."

Father Stephen spoke slowly, as if moving over loose scree. "We are half-brothers. My mother was Lady Maria Doyle from Loch Garan in Eire. I am the product of one of the old Lord Pembrock's extra marital adventures."

"So you're high born. That makes it all the stranger he never mentioned you."

Father Stephen gave a bitter laugh. "Ironic, isn't it? Your father and I would spend all our time together whenever he came to visit Eire."

"So what happened?"

"Oh I'm sure you can guess. I got religion... the wrong sort." Father Stephen gave a tight smile.

When I failed to display either humour or condemnation, Father Stephen said, "What are you after nephew? Do you expect me to confess my blasphemies to a Cigfrân?"

"I'm no carrion crow, uncle. I only wish to understand. I promise I won't betray you. You have my word."

Father Stephen seemed to judge this, then said, with slow deliberation as if each sentence were a chess move, "when I was fifteen, workers uncovered a hoard of ancient artefacts in the grounds of our home. Strange tablets of dark glass bound in metal and what the ancient people called plastique. Mother saw they bore the symbol of the bitten apple, a sign of forbidden fruit, and straight away sent for the priest." His initial caution dissipating, Father Stephen warmed to his tale. "She was a timid woman, afraid of what we'd found but not me, I was fascinated; even in their damaged state I could tell those tablets had been finely crafted and it taxed my imagination as to their purpose. As soon as no one was looking I took one. There were dozens. It wouldn't have been missed."

Deliberately keeping a forbidden item from the Lists of Proscription was dangerous heresy and I asked with barely muted excitement, "Weren't you worried? I was always told ancient teck was addictive, one touch and you would crave it all the more."

"What can I say? I was young but maybe you're right because I did become addicted. Addicted to uncovering the mystery of such things."

The proper response would have been to leave and denounce Father Stephen as a blasphemer. Yet since the incident in the church, my old, blind adherence to the faith was weakening and I was keen to learn more. "What happened to the other tablets?"

"They were shovelled into sacks, exorcised and then burned. Afterwards, they took the blackened remains far out to sea and dumped them... for good measure you understand. Naturally, I took the hint and kept my little souvenir secret." Father Stephen chuckled.

The return of that mocking laugh annoyed me but I couldn't quell the illicit thrill his revelations gave. "Is that when you became a heretic?"

"By Jay, no. It didn't come easy, abandoning what I'd been brought up to believe. That took years of gathering strange relics from those legendary times, some familiar like wrist clocks, but with no spring, while others still defy my understanding. Little by little though, I came to realise how much of our history was missing and how much was invented to fill the gaps."

"So you left the church?"

Father Stephen laughed again, but this time it held a bitter note. "Excommunicated, more like. Banished. Only my high status saved me from a burning. I have little love for the church; it creates *facts* from myths and fragments and destroys what doesn't fit. It is like an ill repaired jar, leaking away our understanding." Father Stephen gestured for the flask but I held off giving it.

"Don't be going back on your word now," he said darkly.

I hesitated and touched mother's wolf-head ring for protection. This was dangerous ground. "My word is good, though I cannot say the same for your beliefs Father Stephen. Are they really worth dying for?"

"I try not to head down that road but tell me, Mathew, would you rather know the truth or to live by a convenient lie?"

"Hah! It is you who debases the truth. Claiming Shambala to be nothing more than a mundane location on earth. It… it's… shallow."

"I never said there was anything mundane about Shambala… or Sambhala as records tell it."

"What records? I've seen of no such records," I said, tiring of this word play.

"Records in the archives of Truro Cathedral in Free Kernow. My order there is dedicated to uncovering the truth of what is and what isn't. They have preserved documents there that demonstrate conclusively that Sambhala was a real place somewhere far to the East by all accounts. Jay or Lord Jayesh, to give him his proper title, rules there with Kasideya Goldeneye. It was a refuge for all true believers wishing to escape the Great Tribulation… and the shackles of oppression," he added.

"That sounds… implausible," I said.

"You are a sceptic. Good. I would hate to think my brother had raised a brainless sheep. Think on this then. Do you really believe that David, your ancestor, actually drove back hordes of Rakshara with only swords, arrows and siege engines before building this wall?" Father Stephen flashed one of his irritating smiles.

Angry I replied, "Of course. I've read the accounts in the Bishop's palace. David the first cleared the land and built the Demonline to protect his subjects. Besides, perhaps they had better guns and explosives back then? I know such things existed before they became hard to replace and the Lists proscribed them. Do you doubt that?"

"Oh I don't doubt he built the wall but the Rakshara were long gone before he even laid the first stone. Beasts or not, they would still have overrun his endeavours, even with *better* guns at his disposal. They are harder to kill than you might suppose." He said this with the arrogance of one certain of his arguments, even if wrong. "No. I say your ancestor reclaimed an abandoned land. Perhaps there were a few scattered beasts that he and his ragged followers managed to overcome but in my opinion, building this wall was a colossal exercise in uniting a people against an imagined foe. As I said, the Church builds convenient truths from myths and legend."

With nothing to counter this, I could only reply, "I don't believe you."

"Well that's your choice." Father Stephen stood and stretched. "I will take my leave. Hunger dictates I seek food but I've enjoyed our discussion. If you are amenable, perhaps we can continue it and uncover the truth together on our journey… nephew." With that he bowed and took up his shoulder bag.

Politely, I returned his bow but my mind ran hot with questions.

THE HERETIC

The sun was sinking into the western horizon and to the east, the Demonline cast a great shadow that stretched for miles. In the distance, the dark woods of the Forbidden Lands lay in a haze, full of dangerous secrets. I had taken the heretic's bait and felt myself being pulled towards those secrets like a herring to a net.

Chapter 9 – A Cloud Across the Moon

It was fully dark by the time I returned for the evening meal.

My companions and I took up benches out near the paddock and when the food arrived we fell upon it like ravenous beasts.

"By Ekata I was ready for this," said Jacques shovelling beef stew into his mouth as fast as it would go. He picked up a corncob from the pile on the sharing plate and began to gnaw.

Tired from the journey and relaxed by the presence of food, incautious thoughts tumbled into speech around the table.

It was Edwin, however who tipped the balance into argument. "Hah! Jack the Rat even eats like one. By Jay, he'll burst before he's done."

"Eh? What did you call me?" Jacques lowered his cob and held Edwin with a narrow, hostile gaze.

"Nothing," said Edwin, embarrassed as his brain caught up with his mouth.

"Is that what you all call me behind my back, is it? I'm a stinking rat am I?"

Flushed red as brazier embers, Edwin picked silently at his food as an uncomfortable silence fell over our group.

With the mood around the table chilling fast, Captain Beech cleared his throat to speak but I beat him to it. "I always thought you looked more like a fox, myself."

Eyes flashing fury, Jacques turned on me, but then like a dropping wind he calmed and a smile graced his lips. "Jacques le Reynard. Bien. I like that. You hear that, blondie?" he growled at Edwin. "It's Jacques Reynard not Jack the Rat. Take care I do not take you by your rooster neck."

The tension broken, they all laughed and Captain Beech passed me a friendly wink, the first of the trip. Finally, I felt I was part of the team.

Captain Beech banged the table commanding our attention. "Right. Before anything else we should outline our plans for the morrow. I propose a leisurely start. We'll use the morning to gather fresh supplies for our journey."

"Gènial! Beaucoup de bière pour moi," said Jacques enthusiastically.

Captain Beech replied plainly. "Yes, *Mr Fox*, but remember your head for the morning and try and limit the damage to your liver. Meanwhile, we have things to discuss so, Mr. Pryce, go find us some more table lighting."

Edwin went to fetch a couple of oil lamps and after checking we weren't being overheard, Captain Beech said in a low voice, "Now Father Stephen, tomorrow we enter the Forbidden Lands. It's time you outlined our mission."

Father Stephen reached into his shoulder bag and pulled out a square of folded material, slightly larger than his hand and a large, stone mustard jar, which he placed on the table.

Tapping the jar, he said, "This is Hide Lotion, as was issued by the Knights of Morn Vale to their supporters in the Great War. In the unlikely event we come across any beast Rakshara, it will mask our scent."

"What about the horses? Will it mask their scent," I asked.

Father Stephen stroked his chin. "Hmm. There won't be enough for them I'm afraid."

"Which would make us susceptible to being tracked. Monsieur L'Ombre. You've been in such terrain before, what hazards do you anticipate?" asked the Captain.

Father Stephen cut in, "There will be very little danger, I assure you. No one has seen a Rakshara since forever and the records at Davidseat indicate no great beast encounters for nearly a century, hence the decline of the Demonline wall."

Jacques replied, "I agree. Great beast encounters are rare but there are other things to worry about. I am wondering if the Father has fully considered other dangers that may lie before us?"

Just then, Edwin returned with two oil lamps and setting them down said, "Guess what? Some *thing* crossed over the border a few miles to the north. It rampaged through a farm, killing the farmer and his son."

"From the Forbidden Lands? When?" said Captain Beech.

Edwin replied, "Just over a week ago. They've doubled the watchtower guard since."

Into the grim silence that followed, I asked, "Do they know what sort of *thing*?"

Edwin replied, "Not as such, though some say it was a giant boar."

"A Hildestvini," said Father Stephen with an air of authority. "Immense creatures used by Rakshara during the Great Tribulation. They are incredibly tough and very strong. Even the Rakshara found them a handful."

"Not good," declared Jacques. "Makes me wonder what other *bêtes maléfiques* are out there?"

"Well, I'd rather be trailed on horseback than have to fend off beasts on foot," said Captain Beech. "We'll take our chances and I'll add a pack mule to our procurement list. Now where exactly are we going?"

Father Stephen unfolded the square of fabric, revealing a map drawn on waxed paper and bound onto cloth. He spread it out over the table. "This I had copied for me from a section of an old atlas in the archives at Truro. It shows Neo Pembrock and a good part beyond. Llys Tywyll is somewhere here." He put his finger on a light green area labelled *Black Mountains* near the edge of the map.

I marvelled at the network of roads and the vanished settlements that had once linked them.

"What do these numbers mean? A40, A48?" asked Edwin.

Father Stephen replied offhand, "The ancients commonly used numbers rather than names for their roads."

"Too many roads I suppose," said Captain Beech.

"Well there are no roads there now. How do you propose finding this place?" said Jacques.

Father Stephen indicated a spot marked *Pen-y-Blaidd.* "The exact location of Llys Tywyll is unknown but this village is mentioned in many tales of walkers vanishing into the hills never to return. I believe this to be our best area to search."

"So, we look for a hidden village, via a village that no longer exists in a land abandoned for centuries. No problem," said Jacques dryly.

"You do realise it could take days, possibly weeks, to search those hills, even if there is anything still left to aim for," said Captain Beech.

Father Stephen's confidence waivered for a moment, then he rallied quickly saying, "It's a big risk but if successful could offer the prospect of fertility to everyone here. You do want children don't you Captain Beech?"

"I am close on forty-five summers old, my time for such things is past, but I wouldn't deny the young their chance to raise a family... if they wanted one." The Captain's gaze rested on Edwin. "Anyway I stink like a tom cat's arse and I'm in dire need of a bath. Gentlemen. I'll bid you a good evening."

"Well," said Edwin. "I could do with a dousing myself after today's ride," and rose to follow the Captain inside.

Jacques sniffed his armpits. "Bah! I too smell like an unwashed whore. I'll never attract a fresh one in this state." Then he too headed off leaving me alone with Father Stephen.

Turning to him, I said, "These Hildestvini, if encountered how best do we defend ourselves against them?" thinking of the exceptional boar my father was heading off to hunt.

"If you are able, it's best to get out of their way," answered Father Stephen

"And if not?"

"Then you die," he said with a chuckle.

Father Stephen bid me goodnight and departed into the night, and I experienced something I'd never felt before. Concern for my father.

Just then, a movement caught my eye across the moonlit yard. Someone was lurking near the entrance, watching me. A spy? With my hand hovering near my dagger, I crossed the yard to investigate.

"Good evening Master Pembrock." A thin man, dressed in Examiner black, emerged from the shadows and touched the edge of his broad brimmed hat.

Suspicious, I said, "Who are you and why were you watching me?"

The man replied, "I am but a poor servant of the church, my name is not important. I gather you just arrived in Caerfyrddin?"

"Yes. We're here on the Bishop's business. I have papers to prove it."

The hat hid the man's face but even so I caught a glimpse of a cruel smile. "Calm yourself Master Pembrock, you are not on trial and I am well aware of your mission. The Bishop informed me you were coming. I merely ask as three of my brothers went missing recently and I wondered if you had heard anything concerning their fate."

I remembered the man called Gren who'd attacked me and whose brother had been burned. However I replied, "No, though we noticed a burning had taken place."

"Ah yes. Two men committed an unforgivable blasphemy against our Great Mother. It would have been remiss of us not to stem their depraved influence would it not?"

I didn't answer but said instead, "Alas, I cannot help with your enquires. So if you will excuse me Master, whomever, I need to bathe."

As I turned to go, the man caught my sleeve, "You are not wearing your Examiner's vestments, I see."

"The road is dusty. I did not wish to soil such holy cloth of the church."

The man nodded, "I quite understand." Then lowering his voice further said, "Oh and one other thing. The Heretic is your main concern but the

Church would be grateful if you would keep an eye on Captain Beech and report back anything untoward."

I replied tersely, "I have seen nothing amiss in the Captain's behaviour."

The man gave a bland smile, "People do not parade their sin, Master Pembrock. Be sharp-eyed, like the raven. We'll be in touch." And with that the man melted away into the night like a cloud across the Moon.

Chapter 10 – The Perspective of the Prey

Still mulling over my strange meeting with the Examiner, I retired to my room and had just removed my cloak when a knock came on the door.

Opening it, I found Jacques leaning against the doorway wearing a sly grin. "Ah, if it isn't *Master* Pembrock."

"Just plain *Mr* Pembrock, or Mat, if you please," I corrected, ushering him in.

Almost lazily, the sharp-faced Frenchman slipped into the room. "Can it be this fledgling has flown the Cigfrân nest?"

"If you mean do I no longer feel comfortable as a Church Examiner, then yes. I just had an unpleasant encounter with one. I lied to him. I couldn't help myself, he disturbed me."

Jacques clapped. "Bravo. I thought you a connard, a fool, back at Caerfyrddin, but now you are learning."

"Learning to doubt myself it seems," I said with a huff.

Jacques grinned. "Well. Doubt is good."

"I'd rather be sure. To know what's right."

"Ah and what is right eh?" Jacques clapped again. "Now. Allez! Come, let us drink."

"I don't feel like drinking," I said.

"Yes you do. Come." Taking me firmly by the arm, he bundled me down to the bar.

Jacques bought us drinks and chatted about his life, fascinating me with tales of his home in Girondeaux, Aquitania where they had electricity and had even revived some ancient teck.

"Is that not against the law?" I said; astounded that teck could be used so openly.

Jacques shrugged, "Different country, different rules. The Septian Church there is far more liberal than your dour Brethon dogma. Does that shock you?"

"It intrigues me. If that's the case, why are you here, scuffing the sand in Neo Pembrock?"

"Life is simpler here. I much prefer the wilder fringes of the world."

Jacques made it sound as if Neo Pembrock were some backward country on a lower branch of civilisation. However given the state of Caerfyrddin I could hardly blame him and let it pass. The evening wore on and I found I was answering more questions than I was asking.

Jacques asked, "So what do you think of Father Stephen and his ideas?"

"I don't know but perhaps he is the only one with a grip on the truth. What about you? What do you think?" I should have been more cautious but Jacques was oddly easy to confide in.

Jacques took a sip of his drink and replied, "Listen, my friend. I am as well travelled as a man can be in this world. I have been confounded by the Turning, hunted monsters and fought the terrible madness of cities. I have travelled as far south as a man can go before the burning girdle of the earth becomes unbearable. Once... and this is the truth... in the scorching heat off the coast of Fuego Iberia I glimpsed the uncanny Alnaar Jinn."

"The Alnaar Jinn?" I said, like some wide-eyed, cave dweller emerging to find a vast new world before him.

"The Fire Lords, whose names are whispered in fear." As he said it Jacques' eyes seemed to burn with reflected fire from the lamps above the bar. "Tall and black- skinned with a silver sheen to their bodies, like metal, though that may be just their dress. I saw five on a spit of land. One of them gestured with his hand and instantly a hot wind took my sails and blew my ship, as if it were a leaf." Jacques let this sink in, then said, "What I am saying, my friend, is we live in a broken world." He waved his arm expansively, "containing more versions of the truth than grains of sand on Pembrock beach. Your Father Stephen does not hold the monopoly."

My head swam with ale and I tried not to slide off my stool. "In that case, which of all those multiple beliefs comes closest?"

"I do not know, but they cannot all be true can they, n'est-ce pas?"

The bar revolved around me, then suddenly everything tipped and I lurched backwards.

Jacques caught me mid fall and said as if from a distance, "Hey steady my friend, I think it is maybe time for you to bed."

"I'm fine." The words stretched out in one long exhausted breath as I clutched at the stool.

"Of course you are. Come, I will guide you back to your room."

Lacking the capacity to coordinate a coherent argument, I let myself be led, puzzled as I couldn't remember drinking that much. By a process of stumbling staggers we eventually reached my room, where Father Stephen's snores could be heard vibrating through the door.

Jacques smiled. "Good luck with sleeping my friend. At least the ale should help."

I snorted and smirking said, "Did you drug me Jack, shack, Jacques?"

"A little. Something to loosen the tongue perhaps. It mixes poorly with alcohol unfortunately but you'll be fine. Are you so very drunk?" asked Jacques, half laughing.

At Jacques' admission I shook the haze from my mind and said with great deliberation, "Not if I concentrate."

"Good. Then listen. Watch out for that one." Suddenly serious, he gestured to the door through which Father Stephen's snores were rumbling. "He is dangerous."

"Dangerous?" I frowned, fighting to concentrate like a drowning man clinging to a raft. "No. Surely he wouldn't betray us?"

Jacques came so close I could feel the man's breath on my face. "I am not saying he would do so intentionally. His sort thinks truth is theirs to command and that always unleashes the most terrible things on the world. Just be sure to watch him, eh?" He tapped his nose. "Oh, and regarding your earlier meeting with that amusing little man in black. Had I found you unwavering in your duty to the Bishop and liable to betray our Captain, then you would be taking a permanent, colder sleep by now." He patted me on the cheek and said jovially, "Think on that eh, Bon nuit," then slipped away down the corridor.

I wanted to believe Jacques was joking but the truth sent a chill shiver through my veins. I had called Jacques a fox in idle humour, but now saw what that meant from the perspective of the prey.

Chapter 11 – Traitors to the Wolf

The pounding on the door punched through my sleeping mind like a forge hammer.

Father Stephen called out, "Kazi, blast and curse it! What in Ekata's name is going on?"

The hammering continued.

"Who's there?" I cried, stumbling from the bed.

I grabbed for my sword but missed as the effects of last night's drinking tripped me.

"Captain Beech, open up."

Head thumping, I lurched to the door and unlocked it.

The Captain thrust his head in. "Grab your things. We're leaving."

"Now? I've just woken up." My head felt like tangled wool.

"Why the sudden rush?" Father Stephen sat up. "I thought we'd planned a leisurely start."

"We did but then a Cigfrân died and now the whole town is in uproar."

Remembering Jacques words, a chill hit me like a dash of cold water. "Was it an accident?"

"He *fell* from the Wall. Does it matter? A troop of militia and Examiners are already heading to Caerfyrddin. Trust me, they'll assume it was deliberate."

Father Stephen grumbled as he pulled on his robes and I asked, "Where's Jacques?"

"Gone with Mr Pryce to gather supplies and, with luck, a mule. The rider who warned me said troops are putting villages to the torch and arresting people all over Neo Pembrock."

"Impossible! Da would never allow such atrocity."

"And what has that to do with us?" said Father Stephen, packing his belongings, "We've got church backing."

Captain Beech gave him a grim look, "Word is we are to be found and detained."

"Detained? Why?" I said. Nothing made sense.

"I don't know. Treason, heresy, take your pick. NOW MOVE! We're wasting time."

Half dressed, half dazed and clutching my pack I hurried after the Captain to the yard where our horses were already saddled and waiting.

"We're meeting Pryce and L'Ombre on the North Watchtower road in half an hour, so no dallying. Now mount up and follow me."

The urgency of the Captain frightened me. It was like a great wave bearing down on us. "Captain, where are we going?"

"To see the rider. He has news you need to hear."

Afraid to ask its nature, I mounted my horse. Then, like a skiff on a racing tide, followed in the Captain's wake with a growing sense of dread.

We hurried through the twisting lanes to a low-roofed house in the shadow of the Wall. Captain Beech rapped three times on the door, which opened a crack and a pale, anxious woman looked out.

"Captain Beech. I have Mathew Pembrock with me."

"Ekata be praised," she said ushering us in.

I was hurried through to a small back room where a man in militia garb stood and bowed as I entered. "My Lord."

My stomach dropped into a pit. No one would call me lord unless... I turned to Captain Beech. "What's happened to Da?"

"This is Corporal Hinks," said Captain Beech. "Tell him corporal."

Without preamble the Corporal said, "My Lord. It is with regret that I must inform you of your father's death."

"Dead!" My world collapsed. "No! It can't be." Nothing could kill Da. It was like saying one had slain a mountain and yet all along I knew this had been my dread.

"A boar took him in the Myntdd forest. Reports say it were a huge beast. No one had ever seen its like before."

My body turned to lead and I slumped into a chair as Father Stephen whispered, "Gruff? Dead? How?"

"You know how, uncle." There was no pretence anymore. "It was a Hildestvini and he didn't get out of the way."

"Uncle?" Captain Beech raised a curious brow.

"Father Stephen is my father's half-brother." I turned to the militiaman. "Corporal, why were those villages burned?"

The Corporal bowed his head. "Beg pardon my lord, but Geraint Skomer has been elected lord. He has the backing of the Bishop and his son Hugh is leading the militia on a purge."

I ground my teeth. "And what of my mother?"

"Be at ease. Lady Constance is safe in Eire."

"And my cousin? Lady Morag?" Be safe, I thought be safe.

The Corporal hesitated. "Lady Morag is to wed Hugh Skomer."

The words sawed into my heart and seized by a fiery rage I leapt up and with a roar worthy of my father, kicked my chair across the room. My mind screaming, *Betrayed!* I clenched my hands into futile fists.

For a while no one spoke, then Captain Beech said, "I dare say she had little choice in the matter."

My anger for Hugh Skomer became a white hot hatred that would have consumed me had I not heard Captain Beech say, "So what now... my Lord?"

Reason regained the helm; I closed my eyes and tried to order my thoughts. "Rally supporters, I suppose. Organise a counter strike, rescue Morag." *Curse you Da for getting yourself killed. Damn your bloody stubbornness.*

"You'll be safe here, for now," said the Corporal.

I nodded rubbing my temples. "Captain, ride and tell Jacques and Edwin we won't be going to the Forbidden Lands after all." My dream of escape ended here. I was Lord now and tied to the land.

Captain Beech sighed, "Actually, I fear the Forbidden Lands are your *only* option now, my Lord."

"NO!" I snarled. "I will not flee Hugh Skomer a second time. D'you hear me!"

"Clear as a bell, but fight him now and you'll lose. Your father made some powerful enemies. You'll get little support here." The Corporal looked aside as the Captain continued, "People might not like the Skomers but they'll pick a strong leader over a weak one and right now they see you as weak."

"Watch your tongue, Beech!" I roared. "My father wouldn't stand for disrespect and neither will I. I'll show them who's weak. I'll crush them like the dogs they are!"

Anger and grief vied within me but Captain Beech faced the onslaught impervious as stone. "Would my Lord like that inscribed on his headstone? Your father hired me to speak plain. Not that he ever took much heed of what anyone said."

Da never listened. That was the truth of it. The storm within me died and I sagged, bereft and becalmed. "You are right. He was an impossible, obstinate man, Jay keep him. Forgive me Captain. I will listen and then decide on our course of action."

Captain Beech put a tender hand on my shoulder and said, "This is the way of it. We go to the Forbidden Lands."

"Captain, you can't…," began Corporal Hinks.

"Quiet, Corporal. No one will track you there and, with luck, we'll return with a cure for the Blight. Then they will rally round you."

"But who knows what horrors lie out there?" Corporal Hinks protested. "Armed men, swords and muskets, these are known risks. You wouldn't catch me facing the demons of those woods for all the gold in Eire."

I thought on this but what the Captain said made sense.

My mind made up, I turned to Father Stephen, "It looks like all our hopes rest on you now, Father. I hope you're right in your assumptions."

Father Stephen replied, "This realm has dwelled in ignorance for far too long. I say we bring it hope *and* enlightenment."

I turned to the agitated Corporal. "Thank you for you service Corporal. It was hard news to bring and the delivering of it may well have put your life in danger."

The Corporal flushed, his eyes flitting to the door. "I'd think hard on your decision my Lord. How can I serve when you are not here with us?"

I smiled warmly. "I will return, I promise, and when I do I will put this land to rights." I looked around the room, fixing in my memory the place where I first heard of my father's death. No mere animal, no matter how huge, could see off Da. It would have to be something truly extraordinary. "Captain Beech. Let's go. The Forbidden Lands await."

Just then, a loud rapping was heard on the front door. The Captain and I grabbed our weapons as the pale woman went to answer it.

Out of sight, a heated exchange took place then to my relief Edwin burst into the room. "Captain! Ten militiamen have just entered town."

"Sooner than expected." Captain Beech frowned.

Corporal Hinks took out a flintlock. "Then stay here. I can hide you."

"Steady, Corporal. Mr Pryce, where are they now?"

"Jacques and I spotted them at the bottom of Main Street. I'd say they were five, maybe ten minutes away. We need to go now."

Corporal Hinks raised his flintlock and pointed it directly at me.

"Drop your weapons. Get in here lad. Nobody else move or I shoot Lord Pembrock here." He called out to the pale woman. "Molly, go tell Captain Skomer I have what he seeks."

The servant hurried away as the Corporal motioned us away from the door.

"Is this how you serve your Lord?" I said, still clutching my sword.

The Captain bid me drop it, saying, "You're no good to anyone dead, my Lord. Have you also forgotten your captain, Corporal? Hugh Skomer will never lead you as true as I did."

The corporal sneered. "My captain? At least Hugh Skomer is a decent man, a proper man, who doesn't encourage his men into filthy, depraved practices. He told me all about you and Pryce here."

"Hold your tongue! The Captain has more decency than you'll ever know." Edwin stepped forward, fists clenched.

Captain Beech forestalled him. "Easy, Mr. Pryce. It's not worth it."

There came a clack and a creak as the front door opened.

"Molly?" called out Corporal Hinks. "Back so soon?"

Molly's tremulous voice came through the door. "Captain Skomer sent a man on ahead. He wants proof you have the one they seek."

With his pistol still trained on us, Corporal Hinks opened the backroom door a crack and called out, "Password."

"To the crow with heretics."

"And traitors to the wolf," he replied, relaxing as he opened the door.

His eyes widened in surprise as Jacques rushed him, sliding his knife under the Corporal's ribs and up into his heart. The pistol went off as he fell back, the ball missing Jacques but hitting Molly square in the head.

"Alas! A poor reward for her password information," he said, as she crumpled to the floor. He took a bow. "But voilà. That's how the fox takes his prey."

Chapter 12 – The Thunder of Hooves

"Keep your nerve, lads," said Captain Beech, mounting his horse.

The rest of us followed suit, trying to pretend to the gathering onlookers that the pistol shot they'd just heard was nothing to do with them. However, the crowd melted away like morning mist at the clattering sound of hooves echoing up the streets towards us.

Captain Beech cursed. "Damn it! Skomer's militia. That way." He pointed to the far street. "We'll try and lead them false, then head back north through the archaeological digs."

"Captain, we've hardly any supplies," hissed Edwin.

Gripping the reins, Captain Beech turned his horse south. "That can't be helped now. Let's just stay alive and get over the border." He kicked with his heels. "GO!"

We broke into a gallop and sped down the street, chased by a posse of barking feral dogs. Scattering townsfolk, I narrowly missed colliding with a cart as we turned first east, then north, weaving our way through the shabby lanes.

My heart beating in time to the pounding hooves, I clung to my horse as it thundered over the hard earth, flashing past merchants and barrow sellers, bakers and blacksmiths, ale sellers and more. I glanced at the people as they leapt from our path. My people now, and here I was abandoning them. Long had I dreamed of leaving Neo Pembrock but never imagined it would be like this.

Churning up a cloud of dust behind us, we left the main town and entered the pitted landscape of the digs. Dodging mounds of spoil and excavations, we raced towards a distant copse beyond which lay the North Watchtower.

"They're on to us, Captain!" shouted Edwin after half a mile.

Glancing back, I saw a second dust cloud in the distance.

"I see 'em," shouted Captain Beech. "Faster, lads, and hope the watchtower guards have not been informed about the change of ruler."

Reaching the copse, we hurtled through the trees to a sloping meadow. The dark wooden stockade of the watchtower lay a short distance below, poised above a wide river valley spanned by an ancient concrete bridge.

"Here we go. Pray our luck holds. Lord Pembrock, you're with me," the Captain cried, urging his horse onto the stockade. With my pulse quickening, I followed.

A cohort of guards, armed with crossbows, approached as we neared the tower and the sound of hammering could be heard from workmen repairing a palisade fence. I noticed they would cast frequent nervous glances across the bridge. It was centuries old standing on cracked pillars, dark with rust and vegetation trailed from its ramparts down to the river. On the far side a vast, brooding woodland marked the edge of the Forbidden Lands.

To our relief, the sergeant in command lowered his crossbow and called out, "That's a mighty hurry you're in, Captain Beech. Not thinking a' crossing over, are you?" He thumbed towards the dark woods. "There's bad things been a'stirring in there."

"Yes, we heard. Did anyone here see the creature?" asked Captain Beech reining in his horse.

The sergeant squinted up at him. "Not a hair. It came through at night."

Straightening up in the saddle, I came forward. "We're here on official business and being chased by rebels. Can you help us?" I handed over my papers from the Bishop.

The sergeant smiled. "Why if it isn't Master Pembrock. Fancy seeing you here."

"Do you think there are more monsters out there?" I asked, with a nod to the far side of the bridge, then glanced back to see if our pursuers had yet reached the trees.

The sergeant flashed a broken toothed grin, "Not my job to speculate but if there are then that fence'll be as much use as a one-legged hound." He lifted the barrier to let us through. "You take care now."

The bridge was like a raised field with a carpet of low scrub and grass and gaping holes where sections had collapsed. Quick as we could we picked our way around these hazards and had nearly reached the far side when Father Stephen called out, "Wait." He rummaged in his travel bag and pulled out the stone jar. "We need to apply Hide Lotion before we enter the Forbidden Lands."

"We don't have time," said the Captain as a far off cry and the thunder of hooves indicated that the militia had broken out from the copse.

Father Stephen held up the jar. "We may not get time later."

Jacques dipped his hand in the lotion. "I agree with the Father. We do not want to trifle with what lies ahead."

"Very well," said the Captain, dipping in, whilst looking back along the bridge.

Father Stephen gave them instructions. "Arm pits and groin should be sufficient."

I took my dip and as we fumbled under our clothes, ten riders reined up at the watchtower and an argument ensued.

"Hurry. They've passed over papers, no doubt authority from the Church," said Captain Beech.

All the guards dropped their arms but for the sergeant who continued to argue until a shot rang out and he fell.

"That's our cue!" shouted Captain Beech. "Go! We'll lose them in the woods.

We sped under the dark canopy and raced left along the edge of the trees looking for an opening.

Our pursuers were nearly over the bridge when we came to a broad gap in the tangled thicket. Leading from it, a ragged trail of uprooted shrubs and smashed trees trailed off into the deep brooding woods.

"Ekata. I don't fancy that," said Edwin with a sour face.

A loud report from behind sent a lead ball zinging overhead.

"There's always the rocks if you don't want the rapids,' replied Captain Beech.

Jacques took the lead. "Follow me and keep quiet. Father I pray your concoction works."

"It will. I'm sure of it," said Father Stephen, ducking as another shot cut through the air.

Cautious and as fast as we dared, we followed the churned path of devastation until we reached a broad open clearing.

Something moved in the dim light at the edge of the clearing and a sharp pungent aroma filled the air. Hearing a deep grunt I froze. Father Stephen had not exaggerated. The two Hildestvini grubbing away at the forest floor towered above us. My horse shied and I gave a silent prayer as two mountains of bristling flesh gave us nothing more than a cursory glance. The Hide Lotion worked, but our way was still blocked.

Suddenly, the militia poured into the clearing shouting, "Surrender, in the name of Lord Skomer."

The Hildestvini's heads shot up at this disturbance and their tails flicked in anger.

"Holy Kazi!" cried the lead man and opened up with his pistol, as did another. Two shots struck home but the boars only gave an indignant grunt, lowered their heads and broke into a charge.

"Scatter!" screamed Jacques as the ground shook before their onslaught. I pulled on the reins to turn but my horse reared and I was thrown to the ground. Flailing, I scrambled quickly to my feet but something caught me hard, driving air from my lungs and flinging me high into the air. A kaleidoscope of trees and sky flashed past and then I was falling, falling, falling.

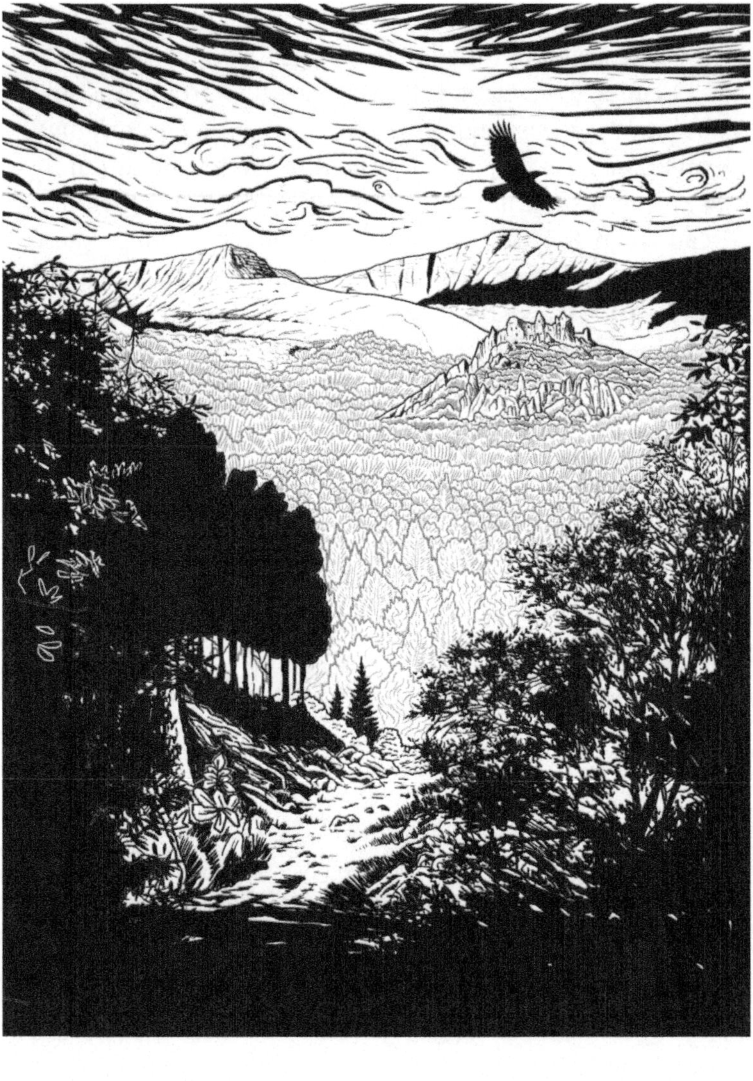

Part 2 – The Forbidden Lands

In the year 2062, having fled Madrid, the forces of Ariadnii, the Spider Queen were harried south by the armies of the Akacha.

Sandwiched between them and the Alnaar Jinn advancing up from Gibraltar, the Rakshara hordes made a last stand in the mountains near El Chorro in what is now Fuego Iberia.

Under the leadership of Nattamara Stormwolf, the Akachan army, known as The Angels of Akacha, fought a fierce three day battle with Ariadnii's Hordes of Rak-Bral.

Nattamara and the Akacha eventually carried the day, with Ariadnii being struck down by fire from the Alnaar Jinn.

However in the closing hours of battle, Colonel Daniel Carrington, the only human officer there, led the Akacha in a charge against a contingent of Rakshara. Although his forces were victorious, Colonel Carrington himself was lost and his body never recovered. It is almost certain he was devoured by the flesh-eating Rakshara.

Thus ended the Great War with the Rakshara and even though the Blight continued to spread for many decades, this is still considered the beginning of the end of the Great Tribulation.

From the archives of the True Heaven Monastery in Truro.

Chapter 13 – A Mournful Deer

I came to, upside down in a thicket of blackthorn. I remembered praying. I remembered the boar and listened for its thunder, but only the bark of a distant fox disturbed the stillness. Wincing from a multitude of pains, I crawled out from the undergrowth to find myself at the bottom of a steep bank, with the woods bathed in the deep golden glow of evening. Tentatively, I felt the raw scrape on my ribs where the boar had torn my tunic. Remarkably, nothing seemed broken.

My belt and dagger were missing, so I picked my way back up the slope to look for them. Slipping on the steep ground, my hand plunged into something cold and wet. I looked down in horror to find my fingers sunk in a pool of gore spilling from half a human head, its one eye frozen in terror at the moment of death. With a strangled cry I lurched backwards tumbling down the bank in a cascade of leaves.

Heart thumping I lay there immobile, trying not to gag as I waited for an attack. When none came after several minutes, I slowly crawled back up the slope.

Relieved to find the half face was not one of my friends, I pressed on to the clearing, where a slaughterhouse of horror met my gaze. Torn limbs, bone, flesh and bloody tatters of cloth lay strewn about. Searching methodically, I worked my way around the gruesome scene, with its split trees and shattered branches. I found my sword next to a dead horse, its neck broken. My own horse with all my belongings on it was nowhere in sight, neither were any of my companions. On impulse, I kissed my mother's silver ring, and thanked Kasideya for saving my life.

With night descending fast and worried by the prospect of the Hildestvini returning, I searched the clearing until I picked up the imprint of fleeing horses. Wasting no time, I struck off after them, pursuing the trail into the woods. When the light became too dim to follow it, I stopped and looked about for shelter. Finding a sandy hollow beneath the roots of an old fallen tree, I crawled into its rude embrace to wait out the night.

Wrapped in the earthy darkness I sniffed my armpits. My application of Hide Lotion was fading and I had no more with me. Hearing strange cries drift through the darkness, I pulled my cloak about me in a gesture that had nothing to do with the cold.

What a catastrophe, I thought, as I considered the scant and unappealing options. If I returned to the bridge, I was certain to be arrested and imprisoned, or worse executed. If I stayed, I had no Hide Lotion, no horse or provisions and only a sword to protect me, which would serve me poorly if the other denizens of the Forbidden Lands were anything like the Hildestvini. *It was never like this in the militia,* I thought. Despite it being Da's idea, I had loved the adventure of it and the opportunity to escape his shadow for a while, until the same hand that pushed me into uniform dragged me back to learn the art of state craft.

Well, I've escaped you for good now, I shouted in my head. *No more will I bear the onslaught of your bellowing tirades.* Yet it seemed a strange, hollow victory, laced with guilt, and I drew no pleasure from it. Why should I miss him dead when I hated him alive? I had no answer.

Such thoughts kept me awake long into the night but eventually sleep stole in...

...I was on a barren hillside. A woman in robes of mist was walking away from me, her face hidden.

"Ma?" I called out but she walked on.

Rain started to fall as I trailed after her down a steep sided valley and I pulled up the hood on the red coat I was wearing. The woman, I noticed, wore the same.

I called out again, "Ma, where are you heading? Have you seen Morag?" But she didn't answer and continued across the barren hillside.

A curious, weather beaten inn, composed of dark timbers and grey stone, emerged out of the haze of the downpour. It had a crazy architecture that made it seem as if several different buildings had been mashed together. The woman in red went inside and I followed after. Cold empty rooms stood either side of a long dim corridor, twisting away into darkness. I passed through a door into a cobbled yard lit by yellow light from a far window. Sounds of laughter and conversation issued from behind a rough door with an iron latch. I lifted it and entered.

"Ah here he is!" bellowed my father, large as life and surrounded by a bevy of evil-looking patrons. "The son who lost my respect and finally my lands. Could anyone in their right mind call this pup a Lord?"

Hot with sudden anger, I cried, "YOU lost them, Da. You soured those who supported us and made enemies of our friends. All I inherited from you was the carcass of your failings."

"Don't dare take that tone with me, lad," roared Lord Gruffydd. In the flickering candlelight I could see a great bloody gash split the side of his head. "Seize him!"

Strong arms took me. I struggled but was forced back onto a table and held down. The woman in the red coat, her face hidden, stood by the bar watching with a black crow on her shoulder. I saw then she wasn't my mother at all.

Even so I cried out, "Help me! Help me!" but she remained impassive as they tore open my coat.

Cruel men leered down at me, their faces hairy and wolf-like, with long snouts and sharp fangs. I fought and screamed but they held me fast and, consumed by terror, I could only watch as they threw back their heads and howled. Then, in the dancing light they pounced, their savage jaws ripping away my flesh.

I awoke with a yell and, cold with sweat, peered wide-eyed into the night. The sky was full of stars and a half-full moon shone through the black branches of the trees with a silver sheen.

"Shhhh," came a voice and turning I saw the woman in red from my dream, sitting on her haunches next to me. Her face remained hidden by the shadow of her hood but her eyes shone out like a multitude of stars. "It's not safe to cry out, Mathew Pembrock."

"You don't want to attract the big bad wolf," said the crow next to her. It reflected no moonlight and seemed a deep, black, empty space.

I rubbed my eyes and found myself alone.

Still dreaming, I thought and lay back shaking.

***

Morning arrived with a feeble dawn whose pale luminescence suffused weakly through the black branches. Slow and stiff with pain, I uncurled and scanned the pockets of low mist for movement. I vaguely remembered a dream and a strange woman but when I tried to recall it the memory became as insubstantial as the mist. Surviving the night and its nightmares brought only a modicum of relief however, for the wild woods were a far cry from the open forests I was used to.

Moving out in an ever expanding circle, hunting for clues as to the path my companions had taken, I found a "V" shaped mark cut into a tree. It brought to mind the secret communications of the militia and cupping my hands I gave a long, piercing bird whistle followed by three shorter bursts.

No answering call came back.

From the V marked tree, horse tracks led off east. Nurturing this small ember of hope, I set off, repeating the call at regular intervals. There were lengthy detours around dense, impenetrable thickets and cooling streams that turned into black bogs with clouds of biting insects. Occasionally, decaying relics of ancient civilisation appeared out of the wilderness. I discovered a concrete pool with black water that emitted a foul acidic odour and later a great rusting frame like the skeleton of some metal beast, half consumed by ivy. Now and again, glimpses of fleet-footed creatures crossed my path but without Hide Lotion to mask my scent I never caught them unawares.

"I wish I had my bow," I muttered, stomach growling as a flock of green parakeets arose from the trees in a flurry of wings and warning cries.

It was near midday when passing through a sea of bracken, I heard a short, deep cough followed by the sound of something large moving towards me. I held my breath hoping it wasn't another boar and gave a sigh of relief when out of the bracken appeared an elegant, broad-antlered deer. It looked at me with uncannily, human eyes, so sad and full of longing that I was beset by an intense melancholy. It opened its jaws, displaying a set of vicious, un-deer like fangs, and gave a bone-searing screech like the screaming of lost souls. Flooded with horror, I turned and ran, with the shriek still raking through my mind. Dodging through the trees I dived into a thicket of holly but the deer bounded in after me.

"GO AWAY!" I screamed pushing and kicking at the vicious tines as the deer tried every which way to skewer me. With branches whipping my face I fell through the holly into a stand of birch saplings and the deer came crashing after me.

Only just managing to evade the cruel lash of its antlers, I stumbled to my feet and sprinted for an old oak. If I could climb up I would be safe but the deer was closing fast. From the corner of my eye I saw it almost upon me.

With a whoosh of air, something flashed past my head and the deer roared. I turned to see an arrow protruding from its flank just as a second arrow struck it in the neck. The deer faltered, then keeled over to the ground.

"Thank Kazi. Bloody thing gave me the tremors," said Edwin riding through the bracken.

I could have cried. "By Jay, Eddie, you're a vision to behold. I could kiss you," I grinned.

"Best not. Captain might get jealous," Edwin smiled back.

"Want to grab your spoils?" I indicated the deer, twitching away.

"By Jay, no. The cursed thing would probably poison us." Edwin reached down to help me onto the horse.

I didn't care, I was rescued, yet as we rode away, the nightmare of the mournful deer stayed with me.

***

"You caught something?" said Jacques, sounding incredulous.

Edwin rode into camp holding aloft the pheasant he'd caught en route. "Yes, and found someone too."

Leaning out from behind him, I waved.

Their faces lit up and all rushed to embrace me.

"Thank Jay. We feared the worst when Jacques found your horse wandering the woods." Captain Beech, gathered me up in a sweat-infused hug.

Edwin grinned. "We're just damned glad you're alive."

"Ouch! Have a care. I'm covered in bruises," I cried, flinching with pain.

"I'll get you some ointment," said Father Stephen with a grin. "Good to have you back."

"Are you a doctor now, Father?" said Jacques with dry wit.

Father Stephen gave him a mild bow. "Like you, I am a man of many talents Monsieur L'Ombre."

We broke camp and not even the downpour that blew in from the west could dampen my spirits. However, several hours of relentless rain dissolved this enthusiasm and the horrors in my head returned to haunt me. I wondered what had gone through Da's mind as he faced down his own Hildestvini boar. Despite all the bitterness between us, it saddened me to think I would never share this experience with him.

I caught up with Jacques and asked, "Do you think we've seen the last of the Hildestvini? The thought of them winds me tighter than a net around a thresher shark."

"I don't know. They were very close to the border, which is unusual in my experience and that concerns me. Normally they keep to the deep woods."

Peering off into the battering rain, I brushed away the water beading on the hood of my cloak. "I'm just glad to see the back of them. Does it matter as long as they are not here?"

Jacques tapped his nose. "Ah my friend, but think what horror could have driven them to the border in the first place?"

"Ekata! I don't want to know! I have enough to fuel for a dozen nightmares as it is." I glanced around nervously.

We crossed a rain swollen river, whose perilous waters buffeted the horses' flanks as they skittered through the powerful flow, then began the long climb up into the mountains. Only once above the cloud-line did the rain finally ease and the dripping woods give way to barren uplands, where heather and dun grass shivered in a stiff breeze.

It was late in the day when we finally made camp in a stand of wizened trees tucked into the shelter of a shallow cwm.

"We should hunt some more tomorrow," said Jacques as he plucked Edwin's pheasant.

"What about things that might hunt us?" Edwin asked. "We must be getting close to this Shadow Court. How do we really know there aren't any Rakshara still out there?"

"The Rakshara are long gone," answered Father Stephen wearily.

"Are you certain?" I asked, no longer certain of anything.

Father Stephen gave me a wry smile. "The Angels of Akacha drove the last Rakshara from the world nearly a millennia ago. The flesh-eating hordes of Rak-Bral no longer walk the Earth."

"Do not speak that name," said Jacques suddenly.

Father Stephen looked up puzzled. "What? Rak-Bral?"

"Do not say it," hissed Jacques, with uncharacteristic discomfort. "It is bad luck." He glanced about as if a horde of Rakshara might suddenly descend from the trees.

Father Stephen smiled, "I didn't take you for a superstitious man, Monsieur L'Ombre."

"I have seen things you couldn't imagine. It is not wise to tempt their wrath, especially when you are deep in their territory."

At this the priest laughed into the night and said, "I don't doubt you have seen much that is incredible, Monsieur L'Ombre, but I have made it my business to separate truth from fancy and I tell you the Rakshara are no more. They are dead."

"Even so," the Captain cut in. "Laugh like that again and I'll gag you. We have no idea what might be listening out there in the dark."

My thoughts immediately went to the strange deer.

Subdued, we ate supper in silence and retired soon after but I lay awake a long time, listening for monsters in the blackness, until the rain returned with a vengeance and drowned out all other sound.

Chapter 14 – Mathew's Call

The next day, under a cold, slate sky, I awoke to damp feet. The previous night's rain had blown under the makeshift canvas shelter and seeped into my bedding roll. Close by, Father Stephen snored away like an old mill wheel.

"I swear to Kazi, I'll take that man's head off one night." Edwin's covers rustled softly as he turned his face from the noise. "How he hasn't called down a horde of demons upon us already I'll never know."

"Well since you are awake now, you can try and catch us some breakfast." Captain Beech was already up and raking over the ashes of last night's fire.

"I'll join you." I wrung out my steaming socks.

Edwin threw off his covers and stretched. "Anything particular you want bringing back?"

The Captain smiled. "Nothing too fancy. Don't go spoiling us with rich food and stay alert. If you see anything dangerous come straight back."

Edwin promised they would.

I took my bow from my pack and joined its two halves together by a leather bound, brass grip.

"Fancy weapon," said Edwin, taking up his own bow and stringing it.

I replied, "Had it made for me. Easier to carry when travelling by coach."

Edwin whistled. "Travelling by coach. My, how the gentry live."

I gave no rejoinder. It was too early in the morning for my still sleeping humour.

Leaving the shelter of the trees, we stalked across the windblown hillside. A hare broke cover from a tuft of grass. I notched and released an arrow in one smooth motion and it struck the hare with deadly impact.

"Damn lucky shot," said Edwin.

I raised a smug grin. "Not luck, just practice. Come now. The bar is set. See if you can do better."

"Right," Edwin drawled, dropping low and working his way through the grass and heather.

A curlew took off with a noisy cry and glided away down the valley.

Tracking its flight, Edwin drew back his bow then stopped. "Hey! Look down there."

He pointed to a large dark shape lying halfway down the slope, beside a whisky coloured stream.

Following his pointing finger, I drew a sharp breath. "Kazi's teeth, it's one of those boars." A change in wind direction brought the unmistakable stench of decay.

"Smells dead," whispered Edwin. "Put an arrow in it and see."

"Not on your life. Let's go tell the Captain."

Slowly we crept away and back to camp.

A little while later, the wind whipping my hair, I waited as Jacques edged towards the carcass. Only the melancholy call of the curlew broke the silence of the hills.

"It is Hildestvini," Jacques called back. "Not as huge as the ones we encountered but still bigger than my horse."

Tilting back the great boar's head, Jacques gave a sharp gasp. "Ekata save us."

"What is it?" called Captain Beech.

"A wolf killed it. A very big wolf."

Father Stephen turned pale and made the sign of protection. "Vukodlak!"

Filled with dread, I looked about the sullen landscape. Of all the Rakshara beasts, Vukodlak were said to be the most deadly.

"We should go back now, while we still can," said Jacques.

"No!" cried Father Stephen. "Look how far we have come already. We've almost achieved our goal."

"Yes and our death too if we continue." Jacques scanned the surrounding moorland. "They hunt in packs. Jay knows how many there are out there."

With his mouth set hard, Captain Beech looked to each of us. "So. What's it to be? Do we return?"

"I would advise it," said Jacques.

"Return to what?" Father Stephen took the stone jar from his pack and waved it in the air. "We have Hide Lotion. They cannot scent us. If we give up now, all our efforts will have been for nothing and we will be hung within the week. Don't you see! We must go on."

"What does Mathew say?" said Edwin. "He's our Lord. He should decide."

All eyes turned to me and the weight of responsibility fell like an anchor, rooting me to the land. Jacques had said Father Stephen would unleash the most terrible things upon us. Yet somewhere in these desolate mountains lay the only hope of a cure for the Blight and any possibility of a future for all.

"What's it to be, my Lord?" asked Captain Beech.

Lord. How I hated that. What had I done to earn it, save get born into a family who gained their noble title by force of arms?

I looked to each of them in turn and sighed. "Call me Mathew, or Mat, or Mr. Pembrock if you will, but do not call me *Lord*. Right now I'm just a fugitive." I pointed to my uncle. "Father Stephen is right. If we go back now we'll hang or burn in a land where towns and people are put to the torch. I desire better than that for Neo Pembroke. We deserve a future where people don't have to watch helpless while their children die, don't you think?" I looked up at the gathering circle of kites, drawn by the carrion. "I won't lie. What lies ahead scares me and maybe we won't find a cure. Maybe we'll all die out here but still I have to try." After a moment's pause, I added, "I cannot ask any of you to do this but I can't do it alone. It has to be all our decision."

Captain Beech looked to Edwin who nodded his assent.

Jacques sighed. "Bien! Fine! I am in. But first we eat. Yes?" indicating the hare I still held. "It is bad to die on an empty stomach."

Chapter 15 – The Shadowed Valley

A few days later, we halted at the head of a pass where a rough track descended through boulders and scree into a valley shadowed with dark and ancient trees.

"This is futile," said Edwin.

Leaning on his saddle, Captain Beech nodded in agreement. "Gentlemen, decision time. We've scoured this land from valley to peak and found no sign of this damned demon court."

"Three days wasted chasing a fantasy," said Jacques.

I scowled and looked down into the valley. It was more than that. I had nothing now to bolster my claim to Neo Pembrock. In my mind I heard Da's mocking voice, *You're a fool, boy, and always will be.* Even dead, he still belittled me.

Father Stephen stabbed a finger at the map. "We must be near. Those ruins a mile or so back had to be Pen-y-Blaidd. If only we had more detail."

"That map is so vague as to be useless," said Jacques, wheeling his horse around to face the group. "I'll say again, we should leave while we still can."

I groaned like a corpse expelling its final breath as Jacques and Father Stephen started arguing and bone-tired from days of riding, my last fragment of hope died in that exhalation. It was over.

"At least we tried," I muttered, more in retort to my phantom father than in reassurance to anyone else.

From out of the barren hills, a thin sound came in snatches on the gusting wind; a mournful howl that faded in and out of the landscape. Others joined it, haunting voices that froze the blood with their chill harmony. My horse shied and gave a nervous snort.

"Merde!" hissed Jacques. "Our luck just ran out."

"So has our Hide Lotion," added Father Stephen. "I told you we shouldn't have used it on the horses."

"And let any creatures out there scent us?" Edwin muttered. "That would never have posed a problem, would it?"

Captain Beech bid them hush. "Listen. The howling is coming from the north. Let us take this valley south. The trees should give us cover until we can turn west for home."

Needing no further encouragement, we hurried down the rattling slope and disappeared into the dappled, dank embrace of twisting trees. Soon bird song replaced the distant howls, yet the tension in the group did not ease. I glanced up at the soaring cliffs, hanging with vegetation. Shining limestone pinnacles pierced the lush forest like the spires of a natural cathedral.

Suddenly, I spotted something. "Jacques, am I mad or is that a window up there?" I indicated where a buzzard circled close to the cliff edge, "and isn't that a wall?"

"By Jay, you could be right. Captain Beech!" Jacques called back.

Father Stephen's eyes lit up when he saw the sure sign of habitation. "Yes. YES! It has to be. Ekata be praised. We've found the Shadow Court!"

"A window in a cliff could be anything," said Captain Beech.

"No. I memorised the description from documents, The Shadow Court lay nestled in the bosom of Ysgyryd Fawr as if born from the very rock. It could only be reached by a flight of rock steps leading up through steep limestone cliffs. This must be it."

"Shame no one thought to mention this Ysgyryd Fawr on your map," said Captain Beech dryly. "Let's look for these steps and hope nothing else awaits us. We're far too crowded out with horrors as it is."

Jacques and Edwin struck off across the wooded slope, keeping as close to the cliff as they could manage, while we waited with the horses.

After a short while they returned and Jacques said, "We found a deep gorge with a river running through it."

"Excellent! Excellent. That must be the way in." Father Stephen clapped his hands enthusiastically.

Jacques replied, "Curb your enthusiasm, Father. There's no way down that we could see. We'll have to continue into the valley and find a more accessible route."

We journeyed on, traversing the hill through dripping woods, until the path opened onto a wide avenue of massive, gnarled and ancient oaks. From there, we traced a vague road back up towards the cliffs. Following the sound of rushing water, we came to a stone bridge over a raging torrent. The air was damp and fresh with the tang of ozone. To one side of the bridge, almost invisible amongst ferns and rampant ivy, rugged stone steps disappeared up into a narrow gorge.

Noting the slick moss and green slime coating them, Jacques said, "We shan't be able to take the horses this way."

"Can't say as I'm keen on leaving them here," said Captain Beech.

"I don't mind waiting," said Edwin, eyeing the treacherous path.

Captain Beech nodded, "Very well but don't try and face down the tide on your own. If anything happens, come find us. Jacques, select ropes, lamps and anything else you think we might need. We find what we came for and go."

I agreed, adding, "The sooner, the better. This whole place blows cold through my soul."

"No argument there," replied the Captain.

Father Stephen was not of our mind however. "We can't rush, Captain. It will likely take more than a few hours to uncover secrets that have been hidden for centuries." Dismounting he headed for the gorge.

The Captain called after, "Hours, Father? I want us out in less than one. Without Hide Lotion we're wolf food if those creatures catch up with us."

"Only if they picked up our scent and followed us," Father Stephen replied, disappearing up the dank pathway.

Muttering curses, Captain Beech and I set off after the eager priest.

On and up we climbed, winding our way beneath branches hung with ferns and moss, our feet skittering on the slick rock, until at last we came to a stone archway. It opened out onto a wide courtyard, choked by scrub willow. Thin grass sprouted from ancient cobbles, like wisps of hair on a balding head and high above, black windows gazed down with sightless eyes. The entrance lobby, a dark and yawning mouth, completed the image.

"Ekata protect us from this madness," muttered Jacques, edging forward to peer in.

"Anything?" whispered the Captain.

I jumped, as with a clatter of wings, two birds flew out and away over the valley.

"Apart from pigeons, it seems deserted," said Jacques.

Captain Beech made the sign of Kazi the Protector. "Swords out, arrows at the ready and keep your eyes and ears open," then he slipped inside and the rest of us followed him into the shadowed hall.

Shafts of sunlight beamed down through the gloom to form pools of light on floors thick with dust, while echoing drips rang through the dank depths as regular as ticking clocks. No other sound perturbed the silence.

"All right, Father. What we are looking for?" I whispered, my eyes darting about, as if some evil creature might suddenly pounce.

"A library. The Rakshara archives were said to be extensive."

Footsteps crunching softly on debris, we made our way down the once grand corridor, its wooden panels warped and stained by centuries of neglect. We found a circular room with tiered seating, where tendrils of ivy spiralled down from a shattered ceiling. In some places, a tree sprouted from the rubble, stretching up towards distant daylight, but as for a library...

"Nothing. Let's try the next level." Father Stephen headed for a flight of stone stairs.

"Easy, Father," said Captain Beech. "I said quick, not reckless."

On the next level, we crept through rooms strewn with fallen rock or decaying wooden beams and sometimes with no floor at all. All the while, the constant drip, drip of water marked off precious time.

Eventually, we discovered what was left of the library at the far end of a dark corridor. Our oil lamps cast dancing shadows over vast, empty shelves and the few abandoned volumes that were left crumbled as soon as they were touched.

"Damn this place and damn the Rakshara!" cried Father Stephen, his voice ringing through the room as he kicked a pile of decayed volumes into a spray of paper dust.

Jacques grabbed him firmly by the arm and pushing a knife against his throat hissed, "Swear more cautiously, Father, or I'll stick you. Remember where we are."

"I'll stab both of you if you don't behave," said Captain Beech. "Father, there's nothing here. It's time to go."

"A cellar. There may be archives below us that we haven't seen, which may have fared better," Father Stephen urged.

"I doubt it. We'll take a look but I want us out of this cursed valley before nightfall."

Returning to the hall, I passed an enormous shard of rock that had crashed through the roof from the cliff above. It stuck from the floor like a huge limestone splinter and behind it, I discovered a hole down to a lower level.

Holding a lamp over the breach, I peered in, wrinkling my nose at the dusty tang that greeted me. "I can see a chamber down there."

Jacques waved his lamp into the hole, illuminating metal cabinets and a dust-covered table. "Seems safe, as far as I can tell."

"I'm going in." Handing Jacques my lamp, I squeezed through the ragged gap and scrambled down the face of the shard.

Jacques passed down the lamp and sword in one hand, I waved it into the gloom as he followed me down.

Two huge white shapes loomed out of the darkness, causing me to cry out.

"What is it?" Jacques called, whirling around and raising his sword.

"Cocoons. Like a spider might make but tall as a man."

One had a tear where a falling beam had struck it and through the rip, a desiccated human face leered out, lips drawn back in a rictus grin.

"There's a dead man in one," I said, holding the light closer.

"Be careful," called Jacques but I was already teasing back the silken threads. As I did so, the body shifted and the frail fabric of the man's ancient uniform ripped revealing a glint of metal. Slowly, I lifted the flat pendant that hung around the corpse's neck and an involuntary gasp escaped my lips, as the name inscribed reached out across the centuries to me.

"What is it Mat? What have you found?" asked Jacques looking over my shoulder.

"Long lost family. These are the remains of my ancestor, Colonel Daniel Carrington."

Hearing this, Father Stephen descended into the chamber.

Pushing past Jacques and I, he inspected the corpse. "By all the saints of Sambhala. The famous Colonel Carrington, hero of El Chorro. What a sorry end for such a legend. I wonder how he wound up here, so far from his last battle?"

"Why would the Rakshara even bring his body here?" I said.

Running his hand over the corpse's uniform, Father Stephen replied, "Oh I'm sure he would have been very much alive. These are Arakni cocoons, made to preserve prey."

Jacques teased at the thread. "For close on nine hundred years? That's a long time."

"Indeed. It was said that people rescued from such cocoons after many decades had hardly aged a day." Father Stephen examined the corpse, tearing the uniform in his haste.

I frowned. "Show some respect, uncle. He's not a grave to be plundered."

"Sentiment won't help us, Mathew. He may be dead but he could still tell us a tale or two."

"Like maybe the location of Sambhala?" I said, indicating my awareness of his true purpose and wondering if my uncle even cared about a cure for the Blight.

"Precisely," said Father Stephen, retrieving a folded wallet from a breast pocket. Brittle fragments of yellowed paper fell from it on opening. "Rats! Just dust and confetti." He tossed it to me. "Here. A souvenir."

It was made of a dull, material, similar to leather but tucked inside, beneath a hidden flap, I discovered two pictures, on paper, if that's what it could be called, for it had an oddly metallic sheen. The first depicted a red haired child of six or seven; the colonel's son perhaps? My however many times great grandfather? The second bore three smiling adults dressed casually in front of a white, sunlit house; a blonde woman holding a chubby child sat next to a short, feral-looking woman with mismatched eyes. A tall, muscular man stood by them, resting his hand on the blonde woman's shoulder. I turned the picture over and my breath caught, for the hand-written inscription read, *Kazi and the Carringtons, Dora, Richard and baby Daniel. Sambhala 2023.*

Kasideya Goldeneye, one of the holiest figures beneath that of Ekata, along with the blessed Saint Dora of Clair. I assumed, baby Daniel was the infant Colonel Carrington. Tears pooled in my eyes, I couldn't speak. The enormity of it took all breath from me as my trembling fingers traced over the images, so human and ordinary. These sacred figureheads, depicted over and over in stained glass throughout the land, were family. My family. For until now Daniel Carrington's parentage had always been a mystery.

"What's getting you so emotional?" said Father Stephen, smiling he held out his hand for a look.

Too stunned to articulate an answer I passed him the picture.

Father Stephen read the written inscription and gasped. "Sambhala. Here on Earth. I was right and this proves it." And yet his lips tightened briefly before handing it back.

He's jealous, I thought. He has no family connection to my mother and therefore no personal link to these sacred icons.

Father Stephen prised open the cocoon a little more. As he did so a skeletal hand slipped out and something slipped from its finger to tinkle on the floor.

"Another family heirloom?" said Father Stephen with derision, as I bent to pick up a silver ring bearing a wolf's head, identical to the one on my own hand.

"Perhaps this is another ancient relative too?" Father Stephen poked at the second cocoon.

"Seriously?" I said, finally finding my voice.

"Let's find out," Father Stephen said with a cold smile.

Just then, Jacques moved between us saying, "You are too eager by half Monsieur. The dead should be left to sleep. I took a look around the chamber and there seems to be a passage leading into the hill. I can't say how far it might go but the air doesn't smell stagnant."

The Captain, who had remained above to keep watch, peered down. "Jacques? Can you come up a moment?"

"On my way." He placed his lamp on a rusting metal cabinet and climbed back up the shard, while Father Stephen began delicately cutting the threads of the second cocoon.

Gradually the silken bundle revealed the body of a woman. Unlike Colonel Carrington, she seemed perfectly preserved. The skin on her angular features, though smooth, bore the finest of wrinkles around the lips and narrow eyes. She had a small, sharply chiselled nose and grey hair, soft as silk. She appeared as if asleep, with nothing to give any indication of the tremendous amount of time she had spent there.

More threads came away, revealing a tawny military jacket with armour-like plates fixed into the fabric and a high-necked, dark grey top with thin red braiding across the upper chest.

"A fellow officer, judging by the cut of these fine clothes. Probably from another regiment," said Father Stephen.

"She's been hurt," I said, gesturing at the puckered red skin on the left side of her face and hand.

Father Stephen took the woman's wrist. "No pulse though. She's dead," then dropped it like a ball of thorns as the *corpse* took a great gulp of air.

Both of us cried out in shock, but when nothing further happened, Father Stephen crept forward and once more took her wrist. "By all the saints. A beat, where there was none before. These cocoons are truly remarkable."

The lips of the woman trembled but made no sound. How tall she is, I thought, and what regal bearing.

Captain Beech's face appeared at the gap above. "Mathew, I need you up here too."

"What is it?" I asked with irritation, reluctant to leave my uncle with the woman.

"Just come and be quiet about it," Captain Beech replied.

Impatiently, I scrambled up and joined him and Jacques, at the entrance.

"Something's up," the Captain said. "The forest birds made an awful racket then fell silent. Edwin just gave a warning whistle."

Jacques whispered, "Can you hear that? The horses are restless."

"I'm going down to Edwin. You two find us another way out of here," said Captain Beech but before he could act, a cacophony of terrifying equine screams shattered the calm.

A moment later, Edwin appeared, pelting across the courtyard as if his life depended on it, clutching his bow and waving his arms frantically.

Captain Beech grabbed him as he shot past. "What is it? What's happened?"

"Vukodlak beasts. I saw them prowling the valley and decided not to wait," Edwin breathed as he nocked an arrow.

"Then that's the end for the horses," muttered Jacques.

"And for us if we don't move. Everyone go! Hide yourselves," hissed Captain Beech, as eerie chattering snarls and snapping barks floated up to echo around the limestone spires.

"Head for the underground chamber," said Jacques. "I think there may be a way out that way."

I grabbed his arm. "What if there isn't?"

"No choice, we're out of options." Edwin pointed across the courtyard as an immense, wolf-like creature loomed into view. It sniffed the air, the grey fur around its muzzle smeared with blood, and its sharp ears flicked. It gave a short, bone- freezing howl then bounded towards us as a second creature appeared behind it on the path.

We raced for the hidden chamber. Jacques reached it first and leapt down followed by Captain Beech and myself. Edwin loosed the arrow he'd nocked and the creature's angry snarl echoed through the ruins.

"Come on, Eddie!" Captain Beech called back from the hole, his voice edged with fear.

Edwin dived, head first, into the chamber. "Did you think you'd lost me?"

His mouth a thin line, the Captain grabbed his arms to pull him through. Suddenly Edwin cried out in alarm, as with a savage growl something took his legs and yanked him back through the hole.

"EDDIE!" shrieked the Captain, as he too was pulled upwards.

"Grab him," cried Jacques.

We all seized Captain Beech and swung from his legs like rags in the wind. Then the Captain gave an agonised scream and everyone dropped to a heap on the chamber floor.

"Dear Jay," I whispered, as light from the lamps revealed the torn ragged mess of the Captain's left arm.

A hairy blood-stained muzzle thrust through the hole, snapping and spraying blood and saliva. I picked up one of the lamps and hurled it at the creature. There was a burst of flame and oil and an agonised yelp.

"QUICK! Grab the Captain and go," cried Jacques, pointing towards the passage.

Instead, Father Stephen seized the woman's cocoon and called for me to help him.

"Leave her," shouted Jacques, as wolf-creatures raked at the hole with vicious claws, showering down plaster and stone.

"NO!" Father Stephen and I cried in unison. "She's alive, she may be important."

Jacques hauled the barely conscious Captain over his shoulder and headed into the dark muttering, "Bloody fools!"

Father Stephen and I grabbed the woman's cocoon and set off after him. Following the flickering lamplight we ran, pursued by the sound of the Vukodlak beasts digging their way in.

"Putain!" cursed Jacques reaching a wide space with several doors leading off.

Through a metal door standing slightly ajar, I detected a slight breeze. "That way," I cried.

Half dragging the Captain, Jacques reached the door first. Its rusted hinges wouldn't budge, but he was able to squeeze through the gap and with my help pulled the Captain through after him.

Father Stephen went next, but the cocoon jammed as we tried to pass it through. A cold sweat claimed me as jabbering snarls echoed down the dark tunnel. "Hurry uncle! Those bloody things have dug their way in."

"Cut her from the cocoon. It's the only way."

Savagely, I ripped away the woman's silk wrapping and heaved her through the narrow gap.

I pushed in after but my pack caught. "I'm stuck!" I screamed and a blood-curdling howl from behind almost stopped my heart.

Father Stephen grabbed my arm and heaved me through as a foul stench of putrid breath clogged our throats. The door shook as something huge and hairy slammed into it, a shower of dust came down and with little warning a massive block fell from the ceiling above.

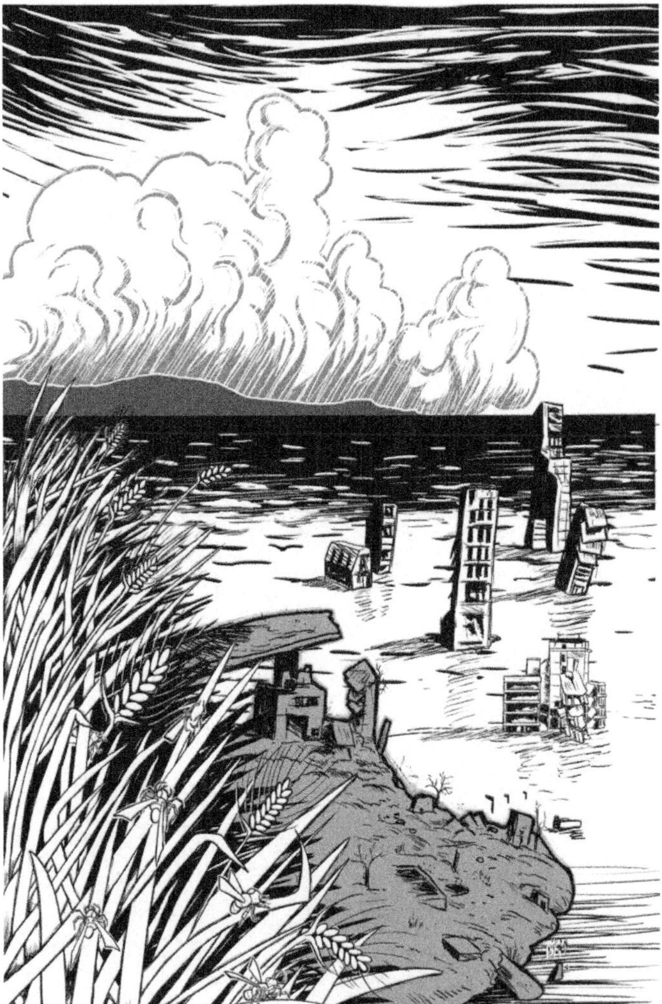

Part 3 – The Madness of Cities

The Ngwag Teg of Y Môr Llwyd
The channel east of Neo Pembrock is much avoided by fishermen, and sailors of that fair land. All would sooner return to port with their holds empty rather than venture into Y Môr Llwyd, the Grey Sea. It may seem a strange title to the visitor, for the waters there are often a beautiful turquoise blue. However, the derivation of the name is from the grey, haunted ruins that pierce the waves and spread like a cancer along the coast.

And not merely on account of these dread structures are the land and waters shunned by all who fear Ekata, for the Ngwag Teg, or the Empty Folk, inhabit this realm and trap any who dare sail into their domain.

Secretive, souless uncreatures spawned from ancient teck they are eternally jealous of the divine spark in man. No one knows what they look like for none who venture in amongst those acursed barren lands and loathsome towers ever return.

From "A history of the curious beliefs of West Europa" by Fleet (2995)

Chapter 16 – A Pit of Bones

I couldn't tell if it were Jacques or Father Stephen who dragged me out from under the huge rock blocking the tunnel. My mind numb, I barely even registered the frustrated snarls and wild scratching of the horrors trapped on the other side.

Stumbling like a drunk, I followed Jacques' dancing lamp down echoing tunnels until we came to an underground river. Stacked under dusty sheeting, we discovered several fibered plastique rowboats, with space for three in each. Jacques declared them serviceable and I was bundled into one, alongside Captain Beech.

"The Captain's bleeding," I said.

"Then do something," Jacques snapped.

In a daze I took the captain's ravaged arm and made a tourniquet from his belt, while Jacques rowed the boat out onto the dark waters. Stupidly, I imagined Edwin was with Father Stephen and the woman in the other boat. *Edwin's gone,* a voice inside me said and I recalled the look of fear on Edwin face as he disappeared. *Don't think of that,* I pushed it down. *Don't think.*

Stalactites loomed out of the subterranean night, lit by the guttering light of Jacques' lamp, as we swept down the dark waters. When the lamp failed, we coasted on blindly, down and down, bumping off walls as we went. At one point, the roof of the channel dipped so low we had to lie flat as the boat scraped and banged against the limestone roof.

We travelled on until time and the world above lost all sense of meaning and I began to wonder if this place would become my tomb.

Eventually daylight came, beginning with a pale dot of green light, which grew larger and larger. Finally, our boats rushed through a mass of vegetation and on into the main river. We swept down the valley, plunging through rain-swollen rapids that took Jacques and me all our sea-learned skill to navigate.

After a while, the river became broader and gentler. We drifted on the current only using the oars as guidance, noting the dark remains of forgotten buildings that peeked occasionally through the surrounding trees. Finally, as the sun neared the western horizon, we pulled onto a gravel bank to make camp.

Straightaway Jacques took charge. "Captain? Captain, speak to me?"

"Damn it, Eddie! Why did you not go before me? I should have let him go before me, Jacques." Captain Beech ground his eyes shut against much more than physical pain.

"That's all on the ebbing tide now. What matters is you're alive, try and stay that way." Jacques searched his pack for medication.

"It's my fault. I should have grabbed him sooner, should have made him go in front of me. I should have…" The Captain slid down the side of the boat, his shoulders shaking as his voice failed him.

Wrapping strips of cloth around the bleeding limb, Jacques said fiercely, "Stop that! Do not think such thoughts. We still need you."

The Captain answered in a hollow voice, "What good am I with this ruined arm?"

"Pull it together, you stoic bastard. You're lucky it wasn't your drinking arm."

"Fuck my arm. I'd trade both to have him back safe." His eyes filled with an immeasurable loss and the stoic Captain Beech crumpled as Jacques held him. Unable to bear the sight of such sorrow, I turned away. *People do not parade their sin*, the mysterious examiner had said back in Caerfyrddin, but there was no sin here, only the losing of someone deeply loved; a pain far worse than the loss of an arm.

Father Stephen came over and whispered, "How is he?"

"Not good," I said, knowing the bandage would not be enough and that the wound was too ragged to be stitched neatly.

"Seems he's taking Edwin's death rather hard. I thought he was a soldier."

To stop myself from punching the priest, I changed the subject. "How's our mystery woman?"

"Weak and delirious. Keeps asking for food. Can't blame her. Imagine going centuries without a meal."

I sighed and stirred myself. "I'll see what we have in the packs."

What we had was very little. Most of our supplies had been lost with the horses and between us there were only two half full water flasks.

Having settled Captain Beech, Jacques took stock of our situation. "Merde! We have nothing! No cooking equipment, no ropes, canvas or sleeping rolls. It's easier to say what we do have." He looked to the sun now touching the top of the far hillside. "There's still some daylight left. Mat, let's you and I go on a scavenger hunt. See what we can find. Here." He handed me my bow and quiver.

"Thank Ekata! I thought I'd lost this in the chamber."

"Weapons are too valuable to lose. I picked it up as we ran but the other bow is lost."

He needn't say more. That bow had been with Edwin.

"Shall I get a fire going?" asked Father Stephen. "I have my pack and a few items."

Jacques rounded on him savagely. "Do what you like but do not speak to me. Ever! Understand? I am laying this cursed mess at your feet."

Suppressing my own guilt, I glanced back at Father Stephen, as I followed Jacques into the woods.

Aware that we could be as much the hunted as the hunter, we hacked our way cautiously through the dense, dripping undergrowth towards a ruined village we had spotted from the river. Crossing an open glade, pale, brown shards crunched and shifted like gravel beneath our feet. Stooping, I picked up one. It was a piece of old bone, pale and curved.

"Human," said Jacques doing the same. "Been here since the Great Tribulation, I imagine. Probably an old Rakshara midden pit." Quietly, he laid the bone back down.

Spurred on by primal fear, I hurried over the rattling bones. "This whole place will devour us."

"Stay strong, my friend. We are dead when we are dead and not before." Jacques patted my arm as he passed by.

On reaching the village, we searched for useful salvage by seeking out places protected from the sun and the elements. Much of what we found was rotten and useless but in the collapsed cellar of a large tumbled-down warehouse we discovered some plastique sheeting and bright blue neilon rope, uncorrupted by sunlight. Such items had often been uncovered at Caerfyrddin and I was always astonished how they remained viable after so many centuries.

"The sheeting will make a good shelter and maybe useful for fashioning a sail when we get to the ocean," said Jacques.

I had already tasted the salty tang on the air. It reminded me of home and the problems that still awaited us. "The Skomer's won't welcome us back, you know."

"Worry about that when the time comes. For now, let's catch ourselves some supper eh?"

I gave him a lopsided smile and nocked an arrow.

***

We returned as light was fading, with our scavenged booty and a brace of grey squirrels. Jacques gutted and spit-roasted the squirrels on some stripped willow saplings, while I checked on Captain Beech.

"We found a little food," I said brightly.

The Captain muttered, "Not hungry."

"No problem. I'll ask again later." Not knowing what else to say, I reluctantly left the Captain and went over to Father Stephen.

My priest uncle was sitting next to the second boat, which he had turned over to make a temporary shelter for the mysterious woman. She lay beneath it, wrapped in his cloak, unmoving.

"Any change?" I said.

"Not much. She's resting now but we spoke briefly on our journey down river. Such a fascinating, archaic tongue."

"Did you understand her?"

"A little," he said, but didn't elaborate.

The sound of shifting gravel alerted me to Jacques's approach.

"We need to leave the woman behind," he said, handing me some cooked squirrel. "I regret having to say it but there is much danger ahead and she will only slow us down."

"Does that also apply to the Captain? Will you leave *him* behind?" said Father Stephen curtly.

"What did I tell you about speaking?" Jacques spat then turned to me. "If it comes down to it I will but only as a last resort. I respect the Captain but I know nothing about her."

"Except that she requires our aid. Why are you so set against her?" I said.

Jacques squatted down beside me and sighed. "In all my years I have always trusted my instincts. Right now they scream deep trouble. The coast lies to the south, not far below us but so does the Drowned City and that is a whole different kind of nightmare. Our only other option is to leave the boats and strike out over land and hope we don't meet any more Rakshara beasts. This will be hard enough without horses, and almost impossible if we have to carry *any* dead weight." He glanced over to the woman.

"The sea would make easier passage. Surely the Drowned City can't be worse than those wolf things?" I said, having only ever heard the Grey Sea spoke of in hushed sailor's tales.

A harsh voice spoke up behind me, "The Ngwag Teg inhabit the Drowned City. That's all you need to know. Nothing living exists there. I've sailed the edge of that cursed sea and seen the strange lights that move in the night and I know that those who go in never return."

"Captain?" Jacques leapt up to tend to him.

"You are right, Monsieur L'Ombre. Mr Pryce... Edwin... wouldn't want me to neglect my duty. I got five people in here and I'll see five people out. Okay?"

Jacques smiled and said, "It's good to have you back Captain."

"Well someone has to stop you and Father Stephen brawling in the dust. What happened happened. We all need to work together now." The Captain allowed a shadow of a smile to cross his face, though it was plain to see the effort it took.

Supper was a sombre affair. Everyone ate quietly, locked in their own thoughts.

Father Stephen produced a cup from his pack and prepared a concoction using water from his flask. "This is an old herbal remedy I use for exhaustion, honey and spices. Sorry it isn't warm. We lost the kettle."

"I'll see about constructing a water basin tomorrow," said Jacques addressing me and Captain Beech alone.

Nevertheless the cup of sweet liquid the Father passed around was very welcome. Even Jacques took a sip. Night fell and a chorus of insects filled the warm air as fireflies lit up the trees.

Jacques took first watch. He promised to wake me some hours later for the second watch but when I awoke at sunrise Jacques was nowhere to be seen.

Chapter 17 – Dire Creatures

"Where's Jacques?" I scrunched across the shingle towards Father Stephen, who was squatting by the river washing his shirt. "He was meant to wake me for second watch."

Leaving off his task, Father Stephen said, "Gone to scavenge more supplies maybe? I've not seen him since first light."

I cast about for the Frenchman and my glance fell on Captain Beech, still asleep, under the makeshift shelter of plastique sheeting. Worried, I headed over. He was usually up before any of us.

The Captain stirred as I shook him.

"Let me have a look at that injury," I said, and he hissed as I teased back the makeshift bandages.

The stump was a torn mess and the arm shredded up to the elbow. I could feel the heat of burgeoning infection radiating off it.

I grimaced. "It doesn't look good."

"And throbs like hell," the Captain replied through clenched teeth. "The wound's infected. I can feel it." He winced as I ripped away the remaining blood encrusted rags and threw them aside.

"I'll clean and cover it but we can't leave it like this."

The Captain nodded weakly. "I know what you're saying. I have to lose the arm or die."

"Sorry."

The Captain shrugged. "It is what it is. Ekata, what a shipwreck of a mess."

"And another thing. Jacques is missing."

The Captain struggled up, his brow creasing. "Missing?"

"Since first light, Father Stephen says. If you ask me, he doesn't seem too concerned about it." I glanced across at my uncle, still scrubbing away at his shirt.

"Well he bloody well should be. I know they don't get on but Jacques has invaluable experience we need. How's cocoon lady?"

"I haven't check on her yet." I shifted my gaze to the up-turned boat. It was angled away from me, so I couldn't see our rescued woman.

With a rattle of pebbles, the heretic priest moved to block my view and stood glowering like a defensive guard dog. "Kazi's claws, I don't know what's gotten into him. He's acting weird like we're suddenly his enemies."

"That man hordes knowledge like a miser. He thinks it give him an advantage," said the Captain with sour humour, watching Father Stephen watching us.

I went to get fresh dressings from Jacques' pack and noticed the Frenchman's sword lying where he'd left it the night before. A frisson of fear coursed through me and I hurried back to the Captain.

"I'm going to go and find Jacques," I said, applying fresh woundwort leaves to his arm. "I can't imagine him going off without his sword."

"I'll help you," the Captain, hissed and tried to rise.

I eased him back. "You're in no fit state. Stay and keep an eye on *him*." I nodded towards Father Stephen as I picked up my bow and headed towards the woods.

With an arrow at the ready, I traced my way towards the ruined village making signal calls as I went but only the forest birds answered. Had Jacques been attacked by some dire creature, I wondered. Or had he fallen and was lying unconscious somewhere? The pit of bones we'd found yesterday played heavily on my mind.

After a fruitless search of the ruins, I left and made my way down to the river. The sun was well up now and the morning mist evaporating rapidly before its heat. I scrambled along the bankside before dropping onto the pebbled shore and followed the river's meandering course back towards camp, calling out as I went.

Rounding a bend, I caught sight of a figure by the water's edge. My heart leapt but it was a woman, not a man. Our mystery woman from the cocoon was awake and looking far healthier than the near dead creature we'd saved the previous day. *Why is she on her own?* I wondered and looked about for Father Stephen.

Appearing not to notice me, she peered at a tablet of glass and metal, similar to the ones my uncle had described back at Caerfyrddin.

I watched fascinated as her fingers stabbed fiercely at the unresponsive device, venting her frustration in an archaic speech I barely understood.

"Izet troo?" she said suddenly, without turning.

My brow furrowed. "Sorry?"

She spoke again as I crossed the clattering stones towards her. "I'm sorry. Your speech hard to understand."

She whirled on me and the sunlight flashed on a pair of dark wrap-round spectacles.

"Talk!" she said, with such command in her voice I had an overwhelming compulsion to obey.

I spoke of how we had rescued her, of my journey through the Forbidden Lands, of my home, my father and more; the words spilling from me in a relentless torrent until…

"Enough!" She raised a hand and I stopped.

Muttering vague curses, she slipped the tablet back into a pocket and slumped down on a washed-up log with her head in her hands. "How long has it been?"

"Since when?" I said, amazed I could suddenly understand her.

"Give me strength. Since…" She seemed to be thinking. "Since the battle at El Chorro. That's the last thing I remember."

"The last battle with the Rakshara?" I said. "Near nine centuries. Give or take,"

"Nine! Impossible! I need proof. Where are we?"

"The Forbidden Lands." I replied.

She looked up sharply. "And where on the Plain of Glass might that be?"

"East of Neo Pembrock?" I said hopefully.

"Last I recall, I was in Spain."

I pointed back to the Black Mountains. "The tunnel we escaped through is back up that valley. Llys Tywyll, where we found you, is somewhere beyond there."

"Llys Tywyll? In Wales?"

"Yes."

"Escaped you said?"

"From Vukodlaks. They… they killed one of our party."

She frowned. "Did they say why?"

"Er, no," I said, puzzled at the odd question.

"Typical!" She looked along from the mountains to the coast, her gaze tracking the descent of the ridge to the barren hillside on their left. "Right. I won't learn anything sitting here."

"Where are you going?" I said as she stood and brushed herself down.

"Up!" She pointed to the crest of the hill. "I need a vantage point."

"It's not safe to be alone out here. One of our party, Jacques, is still missing. I can take you after I find him if you wish."

"I can't wait. We'll look for him on the way. Come." With that, she strode towards the woods. I hesitated but she stopped by the edge of the trees and beckoned me. Deciding it wouldn't do for her to run into some of the creatures lurking out there I checked the arrows in my quiver and made my way towards her.

She kept up a surprisingly fast pace and I wondered how she had become so strong in such a short time. I should have told the others where I was going but there was no opportunity and besides there was something compelling about her, an air of authority that brooked no dissent.

"Who are you?" I asked.

"Who are you?" she fired back.

"I told you by the river. Mathew Pembrock, son of Lord Gruffydd of Neo Pembrock."

"Never heard of you."

"You picked up our manner of speech astonishingly quickly," I said stumbling.

"I have a knack with language. You're basically speaking garbled Welsh mixed with vowel strangled English. It's hardly complex."

We broke through the trees and onto the windblown upper grasslands.

Whenever I could, I continued to fire questions. "Did you fight alongside Colonel Carrington at El Chorro? Were you captured?"

Nearing the crest of the hill she turned to me. "Look, enough of the questions. I'm trying to think. So keep quiet and let me assess the situation."

"If only Daniel Carrington were here. His cocoon was damaged. He didn't survive." I felt the colonel's silver ring nestled in my pocket.

The woman shrugged. "He would still be dead. Those cocoons only slow the passing of time they don't stop it. Look at me. I've gone grey, curse it."

"Then how come you didn't die?" I asked, but she had stopped listening.

With a sudden cry, she slid, kneeling to the ground. I looked past her to the distant ocean, where glistening waves beat against the shattered remains of buildings rising like strange stacks from the bay. On the landward side, other decaying structures spread for miles along the coast, like a cankerous slick of concrete and corroded steel.

"Great Bral. Swansea? Porth Talbot? Surely it can't all be gone?" she cried. "Is anything left of the world I knew? Sea and ruination, it can't all have vanished."

"I'm afraid so," I said. "No cities of the old world remain. All are abandoned, haunted places."

Despite the bright sun, I shivered as the woman sagged and began to emit a low keening cry. A chill wind blew up from the dead city as the keening rose in pitch, and unaccountably afraid, I took a step back.

The woman's shoulders shook as she screamed out into the landscape, "Curse you! Cowards all, abandoning me to a living death. Well Bral damn you to the void and especially you sister, I smell your thread in this. It stinks of your stupid schemes and your stupid plans. Did you think you could shut me away? Did you? Well fuck you! FUCKING BRAL DAMN YOU!"

Her scream reverberated around the hills and surged through me from my teeth to my toes, until I fell shaking to the ground. As if through a haze, I saw her take out her tablet and with vicious force sling it out over the edge of the hill. It spiralled down and down, glinting in the sunlight until it disappeared.

No man or woman could make a cry like that.

"You're not human," I said, my head ringing so I could barely hear her laughing reply.

"Bral's teeth. Have you only just realised?"

"You keep saying Bral, as in Rak-Bral." My blood froze in my veins as realisation dawned. "You're Rakshara."

She turned and removed her glasses revealing cold inhuman eyes as black as pitch. "Oh I am more than that. Much more. I am Ariadnii Jarachini, warrior queen of the Arakni and Magister of the Shadow Court and I'm so glad you're here, Mathew. After a shock like this, I need a snack to calm my nerves."

Chapter 18 – The Pact of Sambhala

Fuelled by terror, I nocked an arrow and loosed it. This close in, even with shaking hands, I could hardly miss.

The arrow flew true, yet Ariadnii caught it with casual ease. "What delightful spirit you have Mathew Pembrock. I so hate a boring meal."

Backing away, I drew another arrow and nocked and let fly. Once again she deflected it. "Oh come on! Is that the best you can do? Would you like a head start? Go on, run, get the blood pumping, eh?"

With no alternative, I turned and fled towards the treeline. Where in hell was Jacques? Surely he would know how to fight this creature.

An image of Father Stephen flashed through my mind. *So the Rakshara are dead are they uncle?* I thought as I raced down hill, gasping and crashing through bracken, leaping over fallen trunks. After several frantic yards, I dived into a dense thicket of holly and froze.

Heart pounding and gulping for breath, I loaded a third arrow to my bow. The wind was blowing towards me and hopefully taking my scent away from the horror stalking me.

If I can just catch her off guard, I thought, though I knew Rakshara were hard to kill. All the stories said so but running would achieve nothing. And so I lay, quaking, like a rabbit hoping to ambush a wolf.

In the still of the forest nothing stirred. *Where was she?*

A crackling came from overhead and looking up I saw a hideous, bloated spider-creature moving slowly through the branches. Pale, like a bloodless corpse, the creature bobbed rhythmically on eight pale legs and four polished black eyes gazed down. "Time's up!" A travesty of a human face grinned, revealing a set of needle-like fangs.

Bursting from my hiding place, I made to run but something struck me like a whip, snagging my legs and spinning me into a tree. The bow dropped from my hand and the arrows spilled off into the bracken. Sticky threads bound me below the torso and snagged my sword. Try as I might, I could release neither it nor myself.

Descending slowly on a silken thread, cracking her joints as she did so, Ariadnii smiled at my predicament. "Bral, it's good to loosen up these rusted limbs. Now don't judge me Mathew. I know two meals in one day is greedy but I am recuperating."

Denied all physical means of defence, I pinned my hope on a last desperate spiritual ploy. Recalling my mother's words before I left, *The Goldeneye ring has protected our family for countless generations.* I thrust my hand bearing the silver wolf ring towards Ariadnii shouting. "Kasideya Goldeneye! I call upon your protection."

To my astonishment Ariadnii checked her advance and cried out. "Oh you have to be kidding me. Of all the Bral blasted humans left on this planet you have to be one of *them*."

Gathering the ring had somehow saved me, I cried, "Yes I am," adding more cautiously, "One of whom?"

"*Amici in perpetuum,* friends in perpetuity. The Pact of Sambhala. Stupid."

A pact? With the Spider Queen herself? I had to know more. "It's been a while, refresh my memory?"

"My, we are in the dark ages. Jay and Kasideya's big, bright idea. Oh we don't want to get involved in your war, let's have a pact instead, to offer assistance and not eat each other and of course, like an idiot, I agreed." She sighed, lowering her hideous spider bulk onto the forest floor. "Never make rash decisions, Mathew, lest they come back to bite you." She narrowed her eyes suspiciously. "So. Tell me how you came by the ring?"

Quickly I replied, "My mother is a descendant of Daniel Carrington, the man whose body was found beside you," though why Lord Jay and Kazi Dayer, the Church's Holiest of saints had made a pact with the arch enemy was beyond me.

"I wonder what he was doing there?" Ariadnii mused.

"You don't know?" I flinched as she drew close but she only used a black claw to strip away the threads binding me.

"You're a lucky man, Mathew Pembrock. Without that ring I would have eaten you." When I made no reply, she added, "You're welcome."

Freed from the binding threads, I started to inch my sword from its scabbard.

Ariadnii noticed. "Don't be getting any fresh ideas, boy. You may be a friend of Sambhala but that ring is no magic talisman. Piss me off and I'll rip your head from your shoulders."

Carefully, I lowered the sword back down.

Ariadnii tutted, "Don't worry, I'll honour the pact. You're safe as long as I don't get hungry." She laughed at my wide-eyed look of fear. "It's a joke! I'm only joking. A shame though, you do look tasty."

She gave a sly wink and I responded with a shudder.

"Now leave me. I need to change back and have a think. We'll talk more later." She dismissed me with an impatient wave.

Needing no further encouragement, I got to my feet, gathered up my bow and arrows and fled like a hunted stag. I thought of nothing, except to beat Araidnii back to camp and hoped against hope she hadn't killed before she left. Two meals in one day she'd said. I thought of Jacques.

***

Father Stephen leapt up, as I stumbled out of the woods onto the gravel bank. "I heard a cry and thought..." My uncle sounded shocked and almost fearful to see me but composed himself quickly. "Did you find Jacques?"

I forced my pounding heart calm. Why hadn't Father Stephen told me about Ariadnii? Something didn't smell right. "No. How's that woman we rescued?"

"Resting. Best not disturb her," Father Stephen replied hastily. "I've just made a herb brew for the Captain. Would you like some?"

With a curt nod, I moved towards Father Stephen. "Here. I'll take it over."

The heretic priest anticipated my intent and coming forward, blocked my view of the upturned boat where Ariadnii was allegedly resting. He held out two wooden cups, one of which had belonged to Jacques.

I smiled without warmth and taking the cups, went to where Captain Beech lay under his shelter.

As I knelt down the Captain said, "Yon bugger's been watching me like a circling shark all morning. I don't know what he's planning but I can practically see his mind turning."

"His plans are darker than we imagined. Here's a brew he made. Don't drink it," I said quietly.

The Captain gave me a searching look. "General suspicions, or something more? I heard a cry up in the hills just now. Did you find Jacques?"

"No but we're in trouble."

"Big trouble?"

"Trapped in a zawn on an incoming tide, but we may yet have a chance. Here." I handed Captain Beech the spare ring that had belonged to Daniel Carrington.

Captain Beech gave it a quizzical look. "What is this?"

"Hopefully a life line." I slid the ring onto the index finger of his right hand.

Captain Beech grabbed me by the shirt and hissed, "Enough with the cryptic hints. Tell me what's happened?"

"Remember that woman we rescued?"

"The one our dear Father Stephen guards so jealously?"

Leaning in close, I whispered, "He's not guarding her. She's up and about. I met her down by the river. She's Rakshara. The bloody Spider Queen no less."

"And my knob can dance the hornpipe," the Captain huffed scornfully.

"Well she turned herself into a fucking huge spider, so pardon me if I give her the benefit of the doubt."

"Fine. She's the Spider Queen. So how come she didn't gobble you up? Reckon she must be hungry after nine hundred odd years."

I gave a thin smile. "That's where the ring comes in. It's something to do with an ancient pact, if you can believe that?"

"I don't but I'll cast off and give it a try," said Captain Beech casually knocking over his cup of herbal brew.

Chapter 19 – As the Night Draws In

Ariadnii arrived in camp just as tensions between myself and Father Stephen broke into open argument. Once more in human form, she emerged from the woods just as I was calling Father Stephen a liar.

"Ah Stephen, lying to our comrades? Covering up my absence? Not doing it very well, were you?" said Ariadnii.

Father Stephen bowed. "Forgive me, Mistress. It is good to see you back."

"Mistress? Why you rotten heretic. I should have let Jacques slit your throat. What did she offer you to betray us?" Captain Beech tried to stand but the effort proved too much and he slumped back down.

I glowered at Father Stephen. "Nothing I'll wager. You did it all of your own freewill, didn't you?"

"Though not without a little subtle persuasion," Ariadnii said, stroking Father Stephen as she passed him.

I shuddered. "What did you do? Enchant him? Drug him?"

"Nothing of the sort. Just an old Rakshara trick. He's a *familiar* now, a servant if you like," then in mock confidentiality, "In truth, I would have preferred the French man but being so weak at the time I had to go for the easiest option."

"I believe I will prove to be a more useful servant than that rough peasant, Mistress," said Father Stephen, with a note of sullen disappointment.

A smile played across Ariadnii's lips. "See. That's how you keep your servants on their toes."

Her presence unsettled me, but somehow I found the courage to say, "Leave and take that traitor with you. There's nothing for you here Spider Queen. Captain Beech is part of our pact. You'll not feed on us."

Captain Beech held up his wolf's head ring, to make sure Ariadnii saw it.

"I see," she said slowly, eyeing me with narrow eyes, then she shrugged. "As you wish. I will honour the pact."

Father Stephen cried out, "It's a ruse. That ring belonged to Daniel Carrington."

I balled my hands into fists and growled, "All the same uncle, the Captain's my friend and therefore a friend of Sambhala."

"Then you must introduce us properly," said Ariadnii, striding over.

Lying beneath his shelter, sweat beading on his brow, Captain Beech looked paler than ever.

"Captain Jon Beech," he said, as her shadow passed over him. "So you are the Demon queen. I have heard about you, mostly from tales to frighten children and warnings to the wicked."

"I'm flattered. Better to be remembered as a ruler of hell than languish forgotten in some forgotten cellar." He edged back as she squatted down beside him. "Don't worry, I won't eat you, even without that trinket on your finger. You're dying and the dying really aren't my thing. I prefer my meals healthy and vigorous."

"Like Jacques L'Ombre?" said the Captain, through clenched teeth.

"Precisely. Though if it's any consolation, he was already unconscious when I fed."

I gave a strangled cry, "May the dark waters take you and your blasted herbal remedy, uncle! No wonder I missed second watch. You drugged us." I drew my sword and advanced upon him.

Ariadnii's voice boomed across the clearing. "Do you want me to save your friend or shall I just let him die from his injuries?"

I halted. "You can do that?" Hope silenced my rage and I lowered my sword.

Ariadnii said to Captain Beech, "If the infection isn't halted you will be dead inside a day or two."

"What makes you so sure? Maybe I'm tougher than I look," said Captain Beech, sweating as he spoke.

She tapped her nose. "Think so? I can smell the poison in you, as well as your fear and anger. I can smell the corrupted Kerun-aki deer creeping around on the far side of this river and I can smell the dangers that lie on the coast ahead of us. Tell me, Captain Jon Beech, do you want your friend Mathew to face those dangers alone, with just us for company?"

"What choice do I have?" the Captain said.

Ariadnii smiled. "We always have a choice, Captain Beech."

He held her black-eyed gaze for a moment, then nodded.

Turning to Father Stephen and me, Ariadnii said, "You two leave. Go and play in the woods or something."

"I won't leave the Captain alone and I certainly won't go anywhere with this traitor," I replied.

Ariadnii glowered. "I need to take spider-form to perform the necessaries. You may not find it pleasant."

"I'm staying." My guts turned to water but I crunched my feet into the pebbled shore to fix my resolve.

Ariadnii shrugged. "Whatever. It's your sanity. Just don't interfere while I'm working. Now, dear Captain, I'm going to put you asleep for a while," and with a speed that defied reaction, she grabbed the Captain and bit down on his neck.

"What have you done?" I yelled, as the Captain went limp.

"What did I say about letting me work?" Ariadnii replied, menacingly. "I've administered a subtle venom. He will sleep for a few hours but it will clear the infection from his blood. Now I will deal with the arm. Watch or turn away, I don't care."

I watched, pondering the paradox of a demon seemingly true to her word. When she started to change however, I had to avert my eyes, not wanting to add any more horrors to my dreams and instead studied my wayward uncle. *How much of this servitude did you want and what was thrust upon you?* I wondered.

After a short time, Ariadnii called out, "There it's done."

The Captain lay asleep beneath the blue plastique shelter. Blood spatters stained the rocks around him but he was clean and his left arm, missing below the elbow, was wrapped in white silken threads. Despite misgivings, some aspect of my tension dissipated.

***

We remained in camp for the rest of the day. The Captain slept and I ate what meagre offerings I found within sight of the encampment. When night came, I took up the watch. It would be a hard task but I would rather a night without sleep than trust my safety to Ariadnii or my uncle.

The evening wore on and eventually Father Stephen retired to bed in his makeshift shelter beneath the boat. Only myself and Ariadnii were left awake. We faced each other across the crackling fire; her pale face glowed ghostly in the flames and her obsidian eyes, glinted with specks of starlight.

"Why did you help the Captain?" I asked cautiously.

Ariadnii stared into the flames. "Old promises are all I have left. The pact was based on mutual help and so I help, besides," she grinned, "there's a shortage of congenial company around here."

A low, mournful cry drifted out of the darkness and I shivered in memory of the uncanny deer encountered on my first night in the Forbidden Lands.

"Do you hear that?" said Ariadnii. "That's the lament of a Kerun-aki turned beast, stripped of all that made it Rakshara."

"How can you tell it isn't some other twisted creature?"

Ariadnii replied, "I can tell the scent of a horned Rakshara and the unclean taint that clings to it. It cries because it is lost without knowing why. It knows it has fallen but it cannot comprehend how far." There was a strange catch of sadness to her voice. "Have you ever felt lost, Mathew Pembrock? Truly lost, as if you were the only person left in the world?"

"Yes," I whispered, my mind going back to that night alone in the forest.

She turned and looked up to where the mass of Black Mountains shut out the stars. "Llys Tywyll was the heart of our culture, the seat of all our laws and the hub of our existence. If it is now a ruin, then what of my people? Are they also dust or did others survive, like me?"

"I cannot say. You are the first demon… I mean Rakshara that anyone has seen in centuries."

Ariadnii squirmed as the mournful cry came again. "Why doesn't it shut its blasted moaning and stop reminding me of what's lost?"

"Tell me of this pact of Sambhala. I don't understand it," I said, to distract her.

"Jay and I helped each other out once, so when our war with the Maun Vaale began, he proposed a truce and I agreed. The Ukachashara of Sambhala would stay neutral and as part of the deal, humans under their protection were off limits. The wolf's head ring was Kazi's idea, in order that they might be recognised. I still respect that."

Angels aiding demons? It hardly seemed credible. "You're saying the Ukachashara were neutral? But didn't they fight you at El Chorro?"

"What makes you think Kasideya fought against us?"

"It's what everyone says." I couldn't accept anything else. Kasideya had renounced the Rakshara. To believe otherwise was a blasphemy too far. "Why would Jay or Kazi ever help you?"

"Revenge."

"For what?"

She gazed into the fire. "Do you have children, Mathew?"

"No," I replied. "Breeding doesn't come easy to us anymore."

"Breeding never came easy to the Rakshara, hence we cherish those offspring we have. I've produced two beautiful sons in my time. The second was still alive last I knew but that was nearly nine hundred years ago and though we live a long time we aren't immortal." As she said it the deer's cry rose up again voicing its grief to the world. "By Bral, I hope he didn't end his days like that."

Abruptly she got to her feet. "That's it. I can't bear this any longer."

"Where are you going?" I said, as she headed down to the river.

"For a walk. I wasn't lying earlier. I'm still recuperating and Bral help me I need food." With that, she disappeared into the night.

I pulled my cloak about me and moved closer to the fire. Father Stephen lay snoring a little way off. My uncle's search for Sambhala had shattered my beliefs, but even he never suggested that our holiest of icons and greatest symbol of evil could join in a pact of revenge.

A little while later, a terrified shriek rent the hot night air and the mournful deer was mournful no more.

Chapter 20 - The Ngwag Teg

In the morning, Ariadnii had still not returned but our previous night's conversation had shown me a different side to her character, one I almost had sympathy for. Almost. All the scriptures said she could be cunning, so I kept some suspicion in reserve. However, having no luck in catching any fish from the river, I decided to risk heading off to hunt for something larger. I judged we were safe from Ariadnii for the time being but I didn't trust Father Stephen, so I went to check on Captain Beech before leaving.

"How are you feeling this morning?" I asked.

The Captain rubbed at his bound stump. "Weak but still alive. I'm not sure our situation has improved though."

"If she wanted to kill us, she could have done so already," I said.

"What if she gets hungry? What happens when we get back home?"

I had no answer to give on those points. "I need to go look for food. I'm hoping to find something with more meat than a brace of squirrels."

"Good luck. I'll keep an eye on things while you're gone." The Captain nodded to where Father Stephen snored beneath the second boat.

Gathering my bow and quiver, I gave Captain Beech a last salute and followed the river downstream. A little way off from camp, I stopped to wash away the night's vigil. A morning mist hung over the waters as I splashed my face but the sight of something near some rocks gave me a greater chill. Jacques' body, trapped like a log in a congested river eddy, his brain case sliced open, empty and half filled with water. My mind numb with horror, I waded through the flotsam and dragged him onto the bank, straining against the weight of the sodden body. It stank of mud and decay, water snails clustered in the ears and other small creatures crawled across the pallid skin. His eyes stared up at me, as if Jacques couldn't believe he were dead. I would have retched had my stomach had anything to void.

Lying on the bank, I waited until the shaking in my limbs subsided before dragging Jacques' body further from the river. In the still morning air I gathered nearby rocks to build a passable cairn around the corpse but in my head an army of thoughts did battle. How long would we be safe? How could we escape her wrath if it came? Finding Jacques was a warning for the future. A red fox emerged from bushes to watch me work, but when I looked up, it disappeared back into the undergrowth.

Finally, I laid the last rock and clasping my hands before me said, "Well Jacques, it's not much but it's the best I can do. You said leave the woman but we didn't listen. I'm sorry you had to pay for that mistake." I struggled to say much more, having not known Jacques for long, but he'd served us well and he'd been right about Father Stephen.

With my stomach growling I headed further into the woods in search of larger quarry, trudging up through the trees until cresting a scrubby knoll. Here, I found myself close to the outskirts of the ill-famed Drowned City. A familiar pungent aroma wafted up the far slope and I dropped to the ground, nocking an arrow as I did so. A few yards below me, six goats browsed in blissful oblivion to the dread ruins around them. Carefully, I calculated the angle, the direction of the breeze and released. With a strangled bleat, a goat fell and at its cry the rest scattered. Most cut off across the hillside but one bounded down, towards an outlying area of shattered concrete and rubble.

I watched it go, bleating as it ran, its hooves rattling over the broken ground.

"Nothing to eat out there little one," I muttered, gathering up my kill.

An odd popping sound reached my ears and drew my gaze to the oily waters of a shallow pool some distance off. In the lea of a concrete wall strange fungi, on branched silver-purple stems, swayed as if blown by a breeze, each branch terminating in a glass-like oval pod. As they popped open, they discharged a cloud of insect-like things. Humming and glittering in the sunlight, the insects spiralled upward then swept from the pool to swarm around the lone goat. I gaped in wonder as faster and faster the cloud of insects spun about the bleating, confused animal. Then drew back in horror as the shimmering purple mass turned crimson and the bleating turned to screams. It lasted barely a minute before the shrieking stopped and the cloud dispersed, drifting like a haze of red smoke back to their pods. Of the goat nothing remained.

***

I arrived back at camp loaded with questions and saw that Ariadnii had returned. Dropping the goat near the fire I took a deep breath and approached her.

"What do you know of the Drowned City?" I asked.

An amused look lit her face. "Why Mathew Pembrock, there's fear on you so strong I could slice it with a knife."

"Earlier you spoke of danger on the coast. What did you scent?"

The amused look faded. "Hot metal and burning grease, sharp odours like needles in the nose. It put me in mind of corrupted nano-tech."

"You mean the Ngwag Teg? Captain Beech mentioned them when we first arrived. Foul spirits that entice men to their doom. What do you know of them?"

"More than you could ever imagine and less than I would like. During our conflict with the Maun Vaale we weaponised many cities, seeded them with AI cyber drones that would continue to fight on our behalf if we no longer could."

Her words were strange, like a foreign tongue and she pronounced Morn Vale oddly, but I intuited their meaning. "Are you are saying you summoned these spirits that haunt the city? If so how do we banish them?"

Ariadnii laughed. "What a delightfully quaint way of putting it. Unfortunately whatever exists in that wasteland will have followed its own course for centuries, continually adapting and changing. I doubt I have any power over it anymore, and besides, not all technology was of Rakshara making. The Maun Vaale developed cyber weapons of their own."

Cider weapons? Her terms puzzled me, but I remembered Father Stephen's Hide Lotion, derived from the Knights of the Morn Vale. Somehow, I had always imagined them in armour, with shields and swords, rather than creators of teck. My view of the world was changing. "Well earlier, I saw a goat reduced to a red mist. Arrows and sword won't defend us against that."

"Then, Mathew Pembrock, I suggest we put out heads together and discuss how to pass safely through their realm."

She walked off but I called after her, "Ariadnii?"

"Yes?"

"Do I understand this right? These things were created from tecknowledge?"

"Yes. I oversaw some projects myself."

"Then how did they survive the Sacred Fire?"

Ariadnii looked puzzled so I quoted from the religious texts. "Ekata stretched forth her hand and drew down her cleansing power. Ribbons of light filled the sky for seven nights and all things made of tecknowledge ceased to function." I still knew my religion, even if my belief lay in tatters.

"Oh *that*. Your history is somewhat muddled, Mathew. The Great Mother's Sacred Fire, as you call it, did much damage but it didn't wipe out every system. It made things harder but hardship breeds innovation and innovation leads to better technology." She glanced at my bow. "Well... sometimes."

We humans ate our morning meal as Ariadnii looked on and outlined our coming strategy.

First of all she laid out what dangers we might face. "The city will have *autonomous systems* for identifying *viable targets,* for instance anything considered a threat or anything considered raw material to be used. Sound, movement, body heat, these are things they may use to detect us."

"That cloud of bugs only attacked when the goat started bleating," I said. "Perhaps their perception is limited?"

"Why don't we travel back along the mountains and avoid the coast altogether?" said Father Stephen.

Captain Beech replied, "That would take at least a week without horses, while a sea journey would only involve a day at most. And there are the Vukodlaks back there to contend with, don't forget."

"I am sure my Mistress could deal with *them*," replied Father Stephen.

"I admire your confidence, Stephen," said Ariadnii, "but the truth is, Vukodlaks, even degenerate ones, are hard to control. It takes time and energy, neither of which I have in abundance at present. I'm not happy about taking the coastal route but Captain Beech is right, it is the best of the bad options."

Captain Beech said, "If we keep mid-stream and give any potential *teck* a wide berth, we might make it. We could also try disguising the boats with branches to make them appear less appealing."

Ariadnii nodded her agreement.

"How are you with boats?" Captain Beech asked Ariadnii. "Can you row?"

She replied curtly, "I have always found others to undertake such mundane tasks whenever I felt compelled to take to water."

Gesturing towards Father Stephen, Captain Beech said with casual sarcasm, "Then I leave you in the hands of this most able sailor. If he scuppers the boat make sure he does it away from us."

"At least I have two hands to man the oars with," said Father Stephen demonstrating his possession of two functioning arms.

Captain Beech glowered at him in silence.

"Well, the sooner we're away the better," I said, slapping my thighs to break the tension.

Grimacing, Captain Beech turned to me and said, "Before we set off, I need to shake this stiffness from my legs. Come on Mat, let's go and leave these two devils to bond or whatever."

With a knowing smirk, Ariadnii watched us stand to leave. "I know you want to discuss me, Captain, but just remember I'm the one who knows what we are up against. You don't."

Captain Beech merely huffed and ushered me towards the riverbank. We walked downstream some distance and as we went I told of my discovery of Jacques' body.

When it seemed Ariadnii was no longer within earshot, the Captain halted and whispered in my ear, "We cannot allow her to reach Neo Pembrock. We have to stop her."

"You mean kill her? I don't know if that is even possible and despite what happened to Jacques she still saved your life. I don't like her or even trust her that much, but I don't think she would hurt us."

"Not yet." The Captain gripped me fiercely by the arm. "Open your eyes, Mat. She's trusting we'll lead her to people whom she *can* feast on. She has to kill to live. You know this."

"I do," I sighed, feeling the weight of the task upon me and knowing full well the Captain's injury would exclude him from any plan.

The Captain was right, of course, we had to do something, but there was still the pact and if I broke that yet failed to slay her I could endanger all who might still shelter under its banner.

"It won't be easy, Captain."

"Killing never is. But understand this; something in that city bothers her. She's afraid, Mat. Perhaps we can use that."

A shudder passed through me at the thought of the crimson cloud. If Ariadnii was afraid then surely it didn't bode well for any of us.

Chapter 21 – An Enemy Worth his Salt

The prospect of killing Ariadnii troubled me, and not just the act itself. I always hated how Da only honoured agreements when it suited him but this was a centuries old pact with an arch demon. I wasn't the one who had made it, so why did the idea of breaking it sit so ill with me?

In addition, accomplishing such an assassination seemed almost impossible, after all this was a creature who could snatch arrows from the air.

The moral and practical problems continued to plague me as the sun approached its zenith and we finalised our preparations to leave.

Father Stephen looked downriver towards the distant coast, "A lot will depend on the tide. If it's incoming we may have to wait to make any headway."

"Well, let's hope things are in our favour," replied Ariadnii. "I don't fancy treading water, whilst whatever lies in wait out there sizes us up."

As Father Stephen moved off I moved in. I'd been waiting for the right moment to tackle the Spider Queen. There was something I needed to say.

"You should know I found Jacques. I saw what you did and gave him a decent burial."

"And you now think me a monster. Is that it?"

"I always knew you were but finding Jacques brought home the reality of it to me."

"Says the man who put an arrow through an animal that hadn't done him any harm."

"That's not the same," I said.

"Isn't it? I was famished. I didn't know or care what his name was. I knew only hunger."

"You found the strength to turn Father Stephen though."

She sniffed. "That took little effort. Why are you telling me this?"

"I wanted you to know I know. So you don't think I'm ignorant of what you are." I had made my mind plain to my enemy and could thus justify any future actions to my conscience.

"Why is it so important I know? What secrets are you keeping, Mathew Pembrock?"

"There are no secrets between us," I said quickly and with a stab of guilt my clarity of conscience clouded.

Ariadnii narrowed her eyes. "I've never lied to you, Mathew. I've got no reason to. But you… you smell nervous."

Trying to maintain a calm countenance, I said, "Jacques once told me he had fought creatures similar to those I saw, the Madness of Cities he called it. He would have been useful."

"Have you ever killed someone, Mathew? A human, one of your own kind?"

"No," I blurted, had she intuited my intentions?

"Last night, rather than consume any of you, I took the essence of a beast Kerun-aki, an animal devoid of intelligence but with enough Rakshara left in it to sustain me. In times past, Rakshara would live off such beasts when humans were scarce and as it was suffering, killing it was a kindness. Even so, the doing of it still left a bad taste." She turned and fixed me with her black marble eyes. "I've killed hundreds of humans, Mathew, and never lost sleep over it but taking that creature's life that made *me* feel like a monster. So I hope you appreciate what I did for you."

I shivered like a hare exposed on a winter field and almost collapsed with relief when she turned and crossed the gravel bank. Seeing Father Stephen greet her my heart hardened towards the heretic priest. *Turned with little effort.* I let that sink in and hate formed around it.

When the boats were packed and scraps of detritus fixed about their hulls, they looked from a distance like floating debris. I lay my ready strung bow next to me and, still wrestling over the unknowable consequences of the task ahead, took up the oars.

One time, I'd accused Da of loving execution, so often did the axe fall but all he would say was, "I don't enjoy it boy. I do it because you never show weakness in the face of an enemy."

I watched Ariadnii draw a cloak of camouflaging leaves about her. She was arrogant and ruthless, just like my father and would do whatever she thought necessary to survive. I had to be like that too but the question was, could I?

Oars dipping and rising, we glided downstream and before long, the river widened out into an estuary. The dark woods on shore gave way to a haunting dereliction suffused with many colours; russet red, twisting iron; pale green and ochre lichen and the dark orange brick of fallen buildings. Scattered amongst these colours were strange pearlescent purples and odd, unnameable metallic tints, shimmering like mirages.

Cutting through the water alongside them, Ariadnii called out a string of unfamiliar names in a whisper that reached my ears as if I were sitting next to her. Solar something, bio-that, I assumed all of it to be dangerous.

Bending in the brine-scented breeze, white skeleton trees lined the shore in a disturbing, alien mockery of nature. Black, ragged things hung from their branches twisting and fluttering as if alive.

The sea, in contrast, was a vivid translucent turquoise, flecked with silver ripples and diamond clusters of sunlight. Glancing over the side, I saw submerged streets and houses. The remains of these and other structures pierced the water in places, while in the pale, blue distance, immense cracked tower blocks dominated the skyline.

By now, the channel had widened into a substantial bay, with the opposing shores some distance apart. It was here the two boats came together and we risked a quiet discussion.

"We have a decision to make," said Ariadnii. "There's an island up ahead and two channels to choose from, both with potential hazards. The left-hand channel holds the greater risk as it involves passing beneath a bridge."

"Why's that a problem?" I asked.

"Something could easily jump us from above," put in the Captain.

"The channel to the right seems clear but there's a kind of *fuzz* on the water that concerns me," added Ariadnii.

"Well, we'd best decide soon," Father Stephen thumbed towards the river. "The tide has turned and the current is gaining speed. If we delay it may pull us onto some unknown hazard before we're ready."

"Agreed," said Captain Beech.

"Stephen, take us over to the right-hand channel but keep it slow. I want to assess what's in the water." Ariadnii crept to the prow and gazed ahead.

With an urgent look from Captain Beech, I tested the string on my bow, its tautness mirroring the tension within me.

As if sensing my hesitation, Ariadnii hissed, "Don't panic now, Mathew Pembrock. Keep your nerve and hold the thread."

I tried to blank my mind and sought some vestige of inner calm as we followed at a distance.

Gradually the strange fuzz gained focus and I recognised the weird fungal growths encountered earlier. Fixed to a collapsed bridge lying just below the surface, these seemed much bigger than those from before and a sliver of a plan formed in my mind.

"Keep us steady as you can," I whispered to Captain Beech.

The Captain nodded and as he sculled with one oar against the current, I took up the bow. Ariadnii was leaning forward now, as Father Stephen slowly manoeuvred their boat towards the translucent pods. Both had their backs to me.

Ariadnii began to make a series of clicks and whistles, long and slow, varying the pitch. When the strange fruiting pods quivered, she held off awhile then started up again with a different sequence, testing the effect. When one sound sequence caused the pods to droop, she beckoned Father Stephen to take the boat in closer, slowly.

The flow of the river was increasing and we started to drift. If I was going to do anything it had to be now. Poised on the tide of consequence, with no idea of the outcome, I drew back my bow and with a long release of breath let fly my arrow.

Ariadnii spun at the whisper of the arrow as it cut through the air. Her hand shot up to catch it but misconstrued its trajectory. She clutched on nothing as the arrow struck home, a boats length short of her, piercing Father Stephen through the right scapula.

With a scream he dropped the oars and clutched at his shoulder.

"You missed!" hissed Captain Beech.

"Shhh!" I urged, as Father Stephen's cries echoed across the water.

With a flurry of rapid pops, the glass-like pods burst open and a cloud of shimmering insects filled the air. Ariadnii slammed her hand over Father Stephen's mouth but it was too late, the swarm headed straight for them.

Careful not to make a sound, I put down the bow and taking up both oars moved our boat further away, though my gaze remained fixed on Ariadnii as she faced the oncoming cloud. The insect-things closed around her, then bulged out as if pushed by an invisible force. My heart stopped, as it looked as if she would drive them off. The swarm surged in once more and Ariadnii forced them back a second time but the glittering creatures regrouped, adapting to whatever she was doing. Once again they enveloped the two figures in the boat and this time they didn't retreat. Red flecks appeared in the spinning, glittering vortex as Ariadnii and Father Stephen beat hopelessly at the swarm.

Then with a scream that cut through teeth, Ariadnii shifted to spider form and burst through the attacking swarm. I followed her trajectory as she leapt high into the air and arced over the water, eight legs trailing. She landed some distance away with a splash and vanished beneath the surface. With the main prize gone, the glittering insects closed in around Father Stephen.

"Is she dead?" said the Captain.

Continuing to scan the water I didn't dare to answer.

Flailing in the now crimson whirlwind, Father Stephen's screams rose in pitch as the cloud of horrors took him apart.

As the heretic disintegrated, Captain Beech muttered, "That's for Edwin and Jacques you bloody traitor."

"We have to go," I said, pulling hard on the oars as more insect-things emerged from the pods and moved towards us.

From the corner of my vision, I saw Ariadnii surface and look straight at me before diving back under the waves. I had broken the pact and failed to kill her. Assuming I survived the next few minutes, I knew she would hunt me down. She was not the sort to forgive, or forget.

Da would have been proud, I mused with dark humour, as the sound of buzzing reached my ears. Such a powerful enemy must surely make me worth my salt.

Chapter 22 – Racing the Storm

The glistening cloud of insects rushed towards us across the waves. I pulled for the left hand channel until the current caught us and we were swept along, like a leaf in a winter's gale.

We shot beneath the crumbling bridge and into a curtain of strange filaments which wound about the boat like animated vines, trapping us in a multitude of writhing threads. A flapping noise from above alerted me and I looked up in horror, as a mass of monstrous, bat-like things detached from the shadowed underside of the bridge. They had hollow maws where heads should be and flew down with cries of "Srkk, srkk" that cut through my mind like nails on slate. I braced myself for impact just as the shimmering cloud of insects caught up with us.

The swarm tore into my flesh but also attacked the filaments, slicing through the tough threads with tiny, silver jaws. With furious metallic cries, the headless bats turned on the swarm, scooping them up like swifts feeding on a summer's eve. I ducked as their wings, flashing like oil on water, scraped the air mere inches from my head as I struggled to free myself.

The battle raged and scraps of wing and insect legs fell like rain as the boat began to slip. One by one, the filament vines released their hold, retracting like springs into the darkness above. Soon our arms came free and drawing our swords, we hacked through the remaining threads until, with a jolt, the boat broke away and shot off down river.

As the enraged shrieks of the fighting creatures faded away behind us, we collapsed, bloody and exhausted, and let the force of the tide carry our boat out onto the choppy waters of the bay.

Our moment of relief was short-lived for a fresh cacophony of harsh cries reached us and we saw to our horror that the boat was racing towards one of several broken towers. I tried to steer away but exhaustion weighed on my limbs and the tyranny of the current was too strong. We gripped our swords and tensed in readiness for a second fight as the immense, rotten structure loomed above us.

No new monsters came to assail us; instead the fractured balconies rang to the cries of a great multitude of seabirds; razorbills, guillemots, fulmars, all species we knew and recognised. Both of us laughed like idiots as our nervous tension evaporated.

The fetid, ancient structure reeked with white excrement and every available space was festooned with arguing birds, each guarding a ragged nest. I shielded my eyes and smiled as I watched them wheel against the sky. The Ngwag Teg had no claim on these abandoned structures, not if seabirds could nest and rear their chicks in safety.

The towers receded into the distance but I didn't allow myself to completely relax until the tide had carried us out beyond the peninsula and beyond sight of the Drowned City. Only then did the impact of my deed hit me, like a dousing wave. "Ekata have mercy on me, Captain, for I've killed my father's brother."

Captain Beech unstrapped the oar from his sore stump. "Don't flay yourself for his passing. That treacherous bastard cast us to the sharks with promises he couldn't deliver on and then betrayed us. And don't give me that *familiar* nonsense either. He knew what he was doing all right."

"Aye," I agreed with some reluctance. Hadn't I also known what I was doing? No one had forced me onto this disastrous mission. I had even assumed the role of a Cigfrân, so determined was I to be a part of it all, in light of which it seemed mean to lay every folly at my uncle's door.

My thoughts turned to Ariadnii. Captain Beech seemed to be healing well, a rare thing in a world where even the smallest scratch could lead to a swift death. Without her help, he would in all probability be dead by now and I had repaid that help by trying to kill her. I told myself it was necessary, the right thing to do, but it still left me with a hollow pit in my stomach. I was certain she wasn't dead and would return to revenge herself upon me, as sure as the tide turned.

A few hours later, the estuary leading to Caerfyrddin came into view. I flexed my aching shoulders to guide the boat as the current drew us in.

"There's a storm on its way," said Captain Beech pointing west.

I watched the curtain of rain slowly approaching from over the water. "And this boat isn't built for rough seas."

"Then pull like the Devil, we don't want it to catch us," he muttered.

And oh what terrible storm have I loosed upon this world? I thought, as the sky above turned black as night and I raced quarter forward across the rising swell towards the estuary and shelter.

***

The first big spots of rain fell as, waist deep in water, we hauled the boat up onto the shingle beach. An old, clinker built, Pembrock Crabber rocked and bumped against a wooden jetty to the left. Tarred and weathered, its halyards rattled in the gathering dusk.

The Captain and I gathered our belongings and hurried through the stinging rain up a narrow path through wind-blown marsh grass to a white stone cottage half hidden in the woods.

We made it just in time. The wind song in the trees grew wild and the storm struck with a roar and driving rain that obliterated the landscape.

"Tyllyr. House of Llyr," shouted Captain Beech above the din and reading a slate plaque next to the door. "Where better to seek shelter from a deluge than the house of an ancient sea god?"

A dog barked within and peering through the rain-lashed window I thought I detected movement.

Captain Beech hammered on the flaking paintwork. "Open up inside! We're drowning out here."

Moments later, bolts drew back and the door opened to reveal a ruddy-faced, white-haired man. He held a loaded flintlock in his outstretched hand and a small dog tucked against his legs snarled at us. Peering suspiciously at the multiple, smeared bloody bites and scratches on our faces he asked, "Who is it coming here creating such an unholy racket? State your business now?"

"Our business is shelter, nothing more," said Captain Beech holding up his remaining hand in a sign of peace.

The man glanced at the swords hanging at our belts. "Is you sure of that?"

"Our intentions are peaceful. Here." Slowly I unbuckled my sword belt and held it out to the man.

He took it but showed no sign of letting us pass. "Trusting sort aren't you. That or desperate. Refugees I take it? I am Dai Ivins."

"Ivins of Tâf valley?" said Captain Beech, removing his sword belt.

"The very same."

"Edwin Pryce told me he had Ivins cousins this way."

The man nodded lightly. "You know Edwin then? I am his uncle, on his dear departed mother's side. Are you friends of his?"

"I am, I was," replied Captain Beech, his voice heavy with sadness.

With the rain hammering on my hood and seeping down my back I added, "Alas he was killed some few days past. Can we continue this in the dry please?"

"Of course, of course. Come yourselves in." Dai stepped to one side and we ducked in out of the beating tempest.

"My comrade lost his arm in the attack. Our sorrow is still raw," I said.

Dai's face fell. "T'is sad news you bring. Keep your weapons. Friends of poor Edwin are welcome here." He returned my sword.

"I'll expect you have come from Caerfyrddin then?" he said, going ahead of us into the parlour.

Captain Beech and I exchanged glances. Had further calamity befallen the town?

Dai collected our sodden cloaks and lighting a lamp bid us sit at a rough wooden table. My mouth watered as a delicious spicy aroma drifted through from the back kitchen.

"Would you like something to eat?" He enquired.

"If it's no trouble," I said. "It has been a while since our morning meal."

"No trouble at all," said Dai, and disappeared into the kitchen.

Immersed in a fug of damp rope and salt-dried fish, I scanned the fisherman's clutter strewn about the room. Nets and crab pots in various states of repair lay stacked about. There were rolled up sails and an assortment of tackle and rigging hung from the ceiling beams.

Dai soon returned with a black iron cook pot and two earthenware bowls. He placed them on the table and filled each to the brim with steaming broth. "Here. Eat. Then you can tell me your names and an account of what befell you."

We devoured the broth greedily and mopped up what was left with wedges of hard bread. Once sated the three of us fell to swapping information.

"How is that arm of yours? Looks nasty. Not infected, I hope?" said Dai.

"It is healing well enough. Have you had any dealings with Skomer's troops this way?"

Dai spat into the fireplace. "A plague on their house. They are the cause of all our troubles."

"It pleases me to hear you say so. I am Mathew son of Lord Gruffydd. Tell us what's being happening? We did not come from Caerfyrddin as you suppose."

Dai squinted at me. "You? Mathew Pembrock? I was told you were killed by boars."

"An exaggeration as you can plainly see," I said.

Dai nodded. "I suppose Eirwen would have said if you were other than you claim."

"And I am Captain Jon Beech," said the Captain. "We have been away and are not privy to recent events in Neo Pembrock."

"Well in the first instance, Geraint Skomer and the Examiners razed Caerfyrddin, put a hundred men and women to the flame they did, and made prisoners of a hundred more. The watch towers were left unmanned and so there was none to warn when the hordes of Twrch Trwyth came and rampaged through the land."

"The Twrch Trwyth?" I said.

"Huge boars of legend, with bristling hides and vicious curling tusks. They laid waste to all before them."

I grew cold at what surely must be the Hildestvini and said, "There is worse to come, Vukodlak beasts from the Forbidden Lands and more."

Dai chuckled and stroked the dog, now sleeping on his lap. "You're a bit late with that news, boys."

"Why? What have you seen?" A chill pierced my soul; surely Ariadnii hadn't made it this far already.

Leaning forward Dai whispered, "For myself, nothing but those who fled Caerfyrddin told of wolf creatures; demons that can bite a man in half and run like a three sky'ler before a squall. They were hunting folk out from whatever hiding place they took to. 'Eirwen,' I said. 'The Day of Atonement has arrived. Best we sharpen up, settle our affairs and stand ready to ascend to Shambala.'"

"Eirwen?" I asked at his second mention of the name.

"My good lady wife."

Captain Beech looked around. "I don't see her?"

"Oh she's about I dare say. Not on this plane mind." On seeing our puzzled faces Dai added, "She cast off the physical three years back, but still lingers about the old place. Sometimes I catch Taygan following her around. I suppose she doesn't want to go on without me."

As Dai went to the kitchen, I hunted for a consoling word to say but nothing came to mind that wouldn't sound trite.

He returned with drinks of nettle tea laced with sloe gin and I asked if he'd news of Morag.

"I've heard she's to wed Hugh Skomer."

"By force, you mean," I said.

"Forced, you say? Folks tell that she and Hugh Skomer have been scheming together for months. They are calling her the cuckoo in the Pembrock nest and I heard tell she carries Hugh Skomer's child."

I choked on my tea. "What? Impossible!" I slammed the table with my fist. "No! I'll not believe this, not till I've heard it from her direct."

"They also say you murdered an Examiner. The church has branded you a heretic."

"Smears and noxious lies," I raged, but then calmed as I remembered how Jacques had disposed of one such examiner.

Taygan gave a wuff and leaping from Dai's knee, ran to the door and stood there emitting a low growl.

My scalp prickled. Had dead Eirwen come to attend our supper? Dai bid us shush and dimming the lamp, slid from the table.

A blast of rain blew in as he opened the door and Taygan whimpered but no apparition crossed the threshold. I joined him in the doorway. The trees moaned like banshees in the wild night but nothing could be seen. Then, through the scream of the tempest came a familiar, chilling howl.

"Vukodlak!"

Shutting the door, Dai snatched up an oilskin bag and went swiftly through to the kitchen. "I hadn't expected them so soon. Grab your things. Quickly!"

Fetching our still damp cloaks and belongings, we found him cramming hard cheese, bread and dried meat into leather bags.

"Do you have water?" If not, fill your flasks from that jug. It's fresh from the well." Dai handed Captain Beech a bag. "Soon as you're ready, let's go."

"Where to?" I asked.

"My boat," said Dai, picking up a lantern, whilst holding Taygan under one arm.

We dashed out into the rain just as another howl cut through the night.

Dai frowned. "Ah! the Divils are close! Quickly now! You'll find long poles on deck to push off with."

Captain Beech ran ahead as Dai grabbed me by the arm. "How are you boys at sailing in this weather?"

I grinned in spite of the danger. "I was born to the sea. This little mist won't bother me." I hoped the churning sea wouldn't take my boast and throw it back at me.

Satisfied, Dai nodded.

We thudded along the jetty, as the howls grew louder through the pounding rain.

Glancing back, I saw vast, dark shapes burst from the steep woods behind us.

"Shit!" I hissed, helping Dai to release the soaked dock lines as Captain Beech jumped on board.

Dai and I snatched up the poles and used them to push the boat out from the jetty but it was a hard task in the buffeting wind and lurching sea. The boat bounced along the line of the jetty but wouldn't leave it.

"Pole to the end," cried Dai, pointing to where the jetty finished. "That is where the current flows fastest.

A cry sounded behind and I saw that one of the wolf demons had already reached the jetty. In a few moments it would be on us.

Turning up the lantern, Dai turned to me. "Look after Taygan. He has good sea legs and won't give you any trouble."

"Dai?" I said, but he had already leapt ashore.

He shouted back, "Go! I'll buy you some time. Can't leave Eirwen on her own now, can I?"

"Dai, she's already dead."

"Mat, come on," cried Captain Beech, as the current snatched at the boat pulling it away from the jetty.

Face on to the charging wolf-thing, Dai cried out in a trembling voice, "Come on you. I'm ready."

I wanted to scream out against this madness but it was too late. The old man brought up the lantern and smashed it down with a burst of flame and I looked away as poor Taygan added his own pitiful lament to the howls of man and burning wolf, then the boat bucked on the raging waves and the shore vanished into the storm.

Chapter 23 – The Son's Return

The storm raged all around but somehow I managed to raise the sail. Through crashing waves and stinging rain we fought to keep our craft afloat, heaving-to when the wind worsened and running with it when it slackened. Captain Beech, lashed to the tiller, steered with his one good arm and kept the bow towards the waves as best he could. Taygan, being used to rough weather from sailing with Dai, sensibly hid in the cabin. Many times our lives seemed lost but nothing would compel me to put to shore and face the horrors lurking there.

Finally, after about two hours, the storm blew itself out. Battered and exhausted, we drifted towards a lone island and sought refuge in its small harbour. A short distance inland, we discovered a ruined monastery and camped for the night in the shelter of its crumbling, thrift-covered walls under a clear, star-filled sky.

"Do you think Vukodlaks can swim?" I asked, looking out across the dark waters to the mainland.

Stoking the fire we'd lit in the shelter of some roofless room, Captain Beech muttered, "let's hope not."

"The creatures wouldn't even be here if we hadn't stirred them up." Shivering I pulled a rough tarpaulin about me, while my clothes steamed on a makeshift rack near the fire. "When all this is done, Captain, you should leave Neo Pembrock. Go and find some peace from all this."

"Hah!" Captain Beech shot back. "Not a chance. I promised your mother I would watch over you and I still hold to that promise."

A thin grin graced my lips. "Then I suppose I must go with you and leave Neo Pembrock to the Skomers. Let them choke on it."

"Now I *know* you are jesting. Fugitive or not you are still Lord of this land. You won't let the Cigfrân or the Skomers ruin it."

My face darkened. "I've not been very successful so far. I'm returning with dire warnings in place of hope, I went looking for a cure but woke a dragon. No one is going to thank me for that."

Awkwardly, Captain Beech pulled his own canvas sheet about him. "Well, thank that traitorous priest for leading us astray. Father Stephen fooled everyone. You, me, the Bishop, even your father."

"Hah! Da would be so furious, wouldn't he?" I allowed myself a fragile grin. "It's the one thing I take comfort from. The old bugger always had to be right, even when he wasn't." Taygan whimpered, so I picked him up and drew him inside the tarpaulin. The dog shivered against my bare skin. "You know, Captain, I've always loved the sea. I wanted to be a fisherman when young, except being the Lord's son, I was bundled off into the militia as soon as I was old enough. Da no doubt hoped to shape me into some martial copy of himself."

Captain Beech smiled. "Don't take on so hard. Lord Gruffydd treated everyone as if they were some extension of his will. I wouldn't say this if he were alive, but he tilled the soil for the Skomers to grow in. If he hadn't alienated everyone they would never have been able to supplant him."

"That's true. Da was a brute and a bully, however, I can't help but think he would have had command of the situation by now. Conflict was meat and drink to him. If only he hadn't faced off against that bloody boar."

Captain Beech huffed, "I'll wager the Skomers had a hand in that."

I stared into the crackling fire a long time, watching sparks fly off into the night.

"Do you think Morag really betrayed us?" I said finally.

Captain Beech shrugged. "Everyone has schemes and ambitions, a way to forward their own ends."

"I don't. I'm not like Da, Captain; I don't have it in me."

"You do yourself an injustice." The Captain handed me a portion of stale bread and cheese. "You may not possess your father's sheer force of will but that don't mean you're not brave. Remember how you stood up to Ariadnii? You think things through like your mother and you have compassion. That's something this land sorely needs." He paused to poke the fire. "Maybe it isn't yet time for that though?"

As I chewed on my bread and cheese, the cloud of bright sparks from the fire reminded me of the Nano Tech creatures that had failed to slay Ariadnii. "Let's say by some miracle we overthrow the Skomers, whilst simultaneously fighting off the Hildestvini and the Vukodlaks. We'll still have Ariadnii to contend with. I cannot think what form her vengeance will take but I expect it will be severe and I can imagine her bending others to her will as she did Father Stephen."

"True. We'll not be able to trust anyone," said Captain Beech, grimly, "and there is no guarantee she won't put us under her spell, now that you broke the pact."

I continued, "Even then, if somehow we win out against her, there remains the Blight. Father Stephen may have betrayed us but seeking a cure was not misplaced. I have to believe there is still hope out there."

"What are you thinking, Mat?"

"That we should continue our search, to Free Kernow and beyond if necessary. Jacques told me the people of West France still use teck in some small measure. They may have medical resources we don't. They may have a cure already, for all we know."

"Fleeing sits ill with me, as you know but returning now would be suicide." Captain Beech's eyes narrowed as he peered into the flames.

I also followed his gaze into the fire. "I agree. I'd rather keep a small flame alive than burn out in a Lord Gruffydd blaze of fruitless violence. Does that make me a coward?"

Captain Beech sighed and looked up into the night. "No. It is the sensible thing to do lad. Live to fight another day. Yet there is one thing we should try and do before we leave."

"Rescue Morag?"

"Aye."

"I agree and besides I need to discover the truth behind these rumours surrounding her."

The Captain looked at me askance, "Although you do realise Davidseat will be crawling with Skomer's troops? And if you're expecting help from the Bishop, forget it. I don't think he likes you anymore."

"Everyone thinks I'm dead, so it's not like they'll be looking for me."

Captain Beech leaned forward. "Then how do you propose to rescue Morag, oh ghost of Mathew Pembrock? Will you rise up from your empty grave to intone to the Skomers their doom and snatch Morag whilst they are quaking in their boots?"

"A nice idea, but no. I'm going to break into Penlan Castle, that's all."

The Captain beat upon his naked legs and laughed so hard that Taygan joined in, barking.

"Oh Mat. Forgive me," he said seeing the rebuke in my eyes, "but that is so like your father."

***

The next morning, we sailed on. The seas remained calm after the previous day's storm and we made good speed. A second night was passed on the island of Ynys Sgogwm, where we shared supper with the lighthouse keeper. The man was oblivious to the turmoil on the mainland and unsure of his loyalties, neither Captain Beech nor I chose to enlighten him.

The following day, a headwind forced us to tack hard until we rounded the last headland, then it shifted to a south-easterly and we raced the current across the bay until the rugged cliffs of Davidseat hove into view.

Spurning the channel to New Port Clais and passing the rocks where Morag and I had once stood, we manoeuvred the boat down a hidden cove.

I dropped sail and used the long poles to coax the boat down between the rocks.

"Careful, lad, don't scupper us," said Captain Beech, as the bows scraped and bumped down the steep-sided cleft.

"I won't," I said casting about with a careful eye. When we reached a narrow ledge, I took up a warp of rope and leaping out, moored up on a protuberance of rock, then secured a second rope to an ancient iron ring.

"I take it you have a plan for wedging us down here?" said the Captain, as I collected a lamp from the cabin.

"Morag and I discovered this place by chance when we were young. We called it our smuggler's cove. At the back there's a tunnel that leads up to the yard of an old farmhouse. From there I can easily slip across the fields to Penlan. Wait for me here. I'll be as quick as I can."

Captain Beech took hold of my arm. "Don't be daft, lad. I can't let you go alone. I made a promise."

"No. I need you here in case anything goes wrong. If I'm not back by next falling tide, you'll know I've been captured."

"Or killed."

I gave a weak smile. "I'm betting they won't do that straightaway. I'll wager the Skomers'll want to make a public display of executing me." A short bark interrupted me. "See we can't leave Taygan on his own, he'll give away the boat, unless you want to infiltrate the castle with a dog in tow?"

Captain Beech huffed. "I could always throw him in the sea."

"I know you, Jon Beech. You won't do that."

"Fine. I'll stay. You have your mother's instinct for people, Mat. I hope it holds for Lady Morag too. Come back safe, else dog or no dog, I'll be coming to get you."

We embraced briefly, then I lit the lamp and disappeared into the darkness at the back of the cove.

Chapter 24 – Morag

I followed the light of the swaying lantern for a quarter of a mile. The tunnel was dank and slippery, freezing water dripped from the roof to seep into my boots as I stumbled through the ink black gloom.

I remembered the adventure of finding this place when Morag and I were children. Happy times. Now the slick walls seemed to crowd in menacingly. What would I say to her? How would I get her away, always assuming I managed to avoid capture myself? The darkness derailed my thoughts and nothing came to mind.

Gradually, the tunnel became drier and the air fresher. Finally, I found myself in a great stone chamber where slivers of light filtered through gaps in the stones. Shouldering aside an old rotten door, I scrambled out through the encroaching grass and nettles.

The abandoned farm surrounding the chamber had decayed further since last I'd visited. Now, it was little more than a collection of moss-covered walls and rotten timbers. Seeing it dissolving into nature installed a pall of dread in me. What if I was too late?

What if the Hildestvini and the Vukodlaks had overrun Davidseat already? Then I caught sight of labourers in an adjacent field and the steady rhythm of their work eased my imagination.

I crossed the fields and scaling the wall of mother's orchard slipped into Penlan Castle grounds. From there, I crept through the garden into the servant's quarters. By a combination of stealth and hiding places known since childhood, I managed to avoid the castle staff I saw. None were faces I recognised; the Skomers had replaced them all.

Armed guards paced the main thoroughfares so I took to the labyrinth of servant's corridors that weaved around the castle. However, there was still one section where they intersected. I would have to cross the exposed main lobby in order to reach the back stairs.

Sliding back a secret door, I peered across the chequered marble floor. The way seemed clear but hearing voices approaching I ducked back out of sight. A moment later, Hugh Skomer and his father, Sir Geraint, hove into view.

"The Bishop is demanding an explanation as to why the Eastern counties are still in turmoil," Sir Geraint was saying.

"Well, the Bishop can look to his Cigfrân for the answer to that. After all, they loosed those bloody boars," said Hugh.

I smiled on learning that the Skomers alliance with the Church was not all cake and wine.

Bitter sharp, Sir Geraint replied, "I'd advise you to moderate your tone, lad. We need the Church on side if we mean to hold this land. Gruffydd may have been a bastard but it can't be argued he kept the peace. This continuing chaos looks bad on us."

"What do you suggest then, Da? The people are beset by monsters and we need to do something. These wolf-things pouring out of the Forbidden Lands are a cursed dagger in our side."

Sir Geraint spat, "Damn it! Lower your voice, lad. Do you want to spread panic? Fire and wolf traps, that's the key. If we could beat them back in old days, we can do it again."

From my hiding place I could hear every word, even their breathing.

Hugh whispered, "and another thing, Da. There's darker rumours abroad. I've heard some say the Vukodlaks are becoming organised, as if guided by some unknown hand. They say people are joining with them."

Immediately, I thought of Ariadnii.

Sir Geraint hissed, "By Ekata, wash that rot from your ears, lad. It swings too close to heresy. You'll be saying the Rakshara have returned next. Yes! That will be it! Heretics spreading lies to discredit us. Well, we'll soon dig them out."

Hugh growled, "That's if the Examiner's fires have left us any heretics still to uncover."

They passed on and the conversation faded. When I could hear them no longer, I slipped quietly across the lobby.

Morag's old quarters on the ground floor were cold and deserted. *Of course she wouldn't be there*, I chided myself. Hugh Skomer would have far grander rooms for his future bride. The sound of a clock chiming somewhere told me it was already two hours past midday. Best to get a move on and try the main bedrooms. I imagined Morag was kept somewhere secure on the upper floor.

Taking the spiral staircase, I stole along the same dusty corridor I'd traversed to spy on Da. It had only been two weeks ago but a lifetime had passed me in that time.

I headed towards my old rooms, thinking Hugh might have taken them for himself and Morag, but passing the library I couldn't resist a peek.

I found the door unlocked and the place ransacked. Books lay scattered everywhere with anything even mildly controversial removed. *Pascal's 'Tales from the Scriptures'*, which I'd read whilst waiting for Lord Gruffydd and Father Stephen, lay on the floor, its pages creased and defiled. Somehow this small desecration encapsulated my contempt for the Skomers.

"Uneducated thugs," I muttered. Da was a saint in comparison.

Pressing my ear to the fake bookcase and hearing no sound, I cautiously opened the hidden door to father's study and gasped. Morag, who had been quietly reading, looked up her face turning pale as she saw me.

She opened her mouth but I put a finger to my lips and said quietly, "Shhh. I'm no ghost."

"We thought you dead, killed by the great boars," she said rushing to embrace me.

I revelled in her warmth then noted the slight swelling of her belly and something inside of me died. How naïve was I to have attributed it to good food? "Damn it, Morag! How long have you played me for a fool?"

"It wasn't out of choice, believe me." She pulled back and looked me in the eye. "My position was precarious and your father's days were shortening. Even Lady Constance knew that. I had to do something to ensure my survival for when it all fell apart. I've been cultivating Hugh Skomer for a while."

"How terrible for you. It must have been a real struggle to breath under the great weight of Hugh's belly."

Cold as slate, Morag pushed me away. "Did you come back from the dead just to call me a slattern?"

"I came to rescue you," I said, my anger rising.

"I thought you were bringing a cure for the Blight?"

"There is no cure for the Blight. We found nothing but dust."

"What a surprise. Your pointless little trip didn't deliver." Morag stroked her belly. "This isn't dust though. Children are currency, you know that, Mat."

Soured by anger I said, "You've been pregnant before, remember?"

I regretted the words as soon as they loosed.

Their arrows struck deep and Morag cried out, "Damn you, Mathew Pembrock. By Kazi, the Forbidden Lands have made you cruel."

I flushed but stood my ground. "I could say the same of you but perhaps you were always that way."

"At least I didn't join the damned Cigfrân." Morag spat. "You sided with those thugs just to get what you wanted and to the rocks with anyone else."

That skewered my pride. "I've come to regret that now. I didn't understand the Examiners at the time, or what they stood for."

Morag's anger faded and she took my hand. "Truly, I never wanted to hurt you, Mat. I like being your friend but don't you see? It's hard for women like me when power is filtered through men. Lady Constance should have ruled this land but Lord Gruffydd always had to have the final say. I don't want to be in anyone's shadow, neither yours nor Hugh's."

I smiled wanly. "I get that. Da was always trying to press me into the mould of a fighter and I hated it." A shadow passed over me as I recalled the death of Father Stephen. "Yet we can't always escape what the world forces us to be."

"What sort of useless phrase is that, when people like your father and Sir Geraint glorify war and murder as a necessity for good leadership? You would think we'd have learned by now."

A melancholy air settled between us.

I knew I had to do what was right. "Come with me, Mog. It's too dangerous to stay here."

"If you mean the Hildestvini and the Vukodlaks, we already know of them. They're causing chaos in the east."

"Not the Vukodlaks, something much worse. There's a storm on the way and it's called…" but I never finished, for at that moment the study door was throw open and Hugh Skomer stood in the frame.

"Ho! I thought I heard dog bark and here it is. Looking good for a dead man, Mat. Come to turn yourself in?"

Hugh reached for his sword as I drew my knife and put myself between him and Morag. "Back off, Hugh. I only came for Morag and to warn you."

Hugh held his sword lightly with expert ease. "You? Warn me? I see you kept your sense of humour then. Save the fancy speeches for the gallows, Mat, or do you prefer the fire?"

I edged back towards the opening of the hidden door. "I'd love to stay and reminisce, Hugh, but time is pressing. Pardon me if we take our leave."

Something cold pressed against my neck. "I'm afraid you won't be going anywhere, Mat. Drop the knife."

I let my dagger fall as Morag pushed hers against my flesh. "Forgive me but old friendships are too costly to maintain these days."

Chapter 25 – The Ebbing Tide

I awoke with my face pressed against a cold stone floor and a stale reek of urine in my nostrils. I tried to rise but a spasm of agony cut short the effort. When the pain subsided I tried again and with incremental stiffness edged myself upright. The filthy, straw-covered floor, the grey stone walls weeping tears of glistening slime and the cries of others echoing through black-iron bars confirmed my fears. I was a prisoner in Penlan dungeon. I'd visited a few times with Da, but this new perspective was far from welcome. Golden light from a high barred window indicated evening and the hours of consciousness I'd missed.

Tentatively, I assessed my battered body. I had a broken nose and my right eye was swollen but though I ached with hidden bruises I didn't seem to have suffered any major damage, a surprise after the beating I'd taken in the yard. Hugh needed to show who was in charge and at least they'd read me the list of charges first; Treason, heresy, avoiding quarantine, reckless endangerment of the population. I expected more would be added later.

"Well done, Mathew," I said out loud, the sound of my voice dropping dead in the air. "That couldn't have gone worse if you'd tried."

Hugh had laughed at my warning, the idiot. He found the idea of a powerful Rakshara coming to usurp him ridiculous.

"Your mind's been deformed by that heretic, Mat, else you think me a bigger fool than you are," he scoffed, then he and his guards laid into me.

As the last rays of light faded, my thoughts ran to Captain Beech. Was he still waiting? I couldn't see how on earth he could extract me from this mess.

A little later the guards changed shift. Grumbling greetings to each other, one gave a cruel hearty laugh and said in the local Welsh lilt, "Shall I be telling him or shall you?"

"Your news, Gam. You tell 'im," said the other.

Footsteps accompanied by a swinging lantern approached my cell.

The guard's uneven teeth glinted in its flickering light. "Master Pembrock," he said in mocking tone, "I've news for you. The militia discovered that boat of yours. They knew it were you, see, 'cause they found your fancy bow after they killed your mate." Having delivered these wounding words, he bowed and mocking said, "You have yourself a nice evening now."

I clenched my teeth against the urge to cry out, determined not to let my torment show. I wouldn't give these bastards the satisfaction, yet as night deepened a cruel emptiness took hold of me. Edwin,

Jacques, Father Stephen, Dai and now Captain Beech, all dead by my folly, with nothing to show for it. In despair I prayed for execution to come and usher me from this friendless world.

The pitiful cries of prisoners faded as sleep took them, leaving only the sound of dripping water, scurrying rats and the rude snoring of my gaoler.

I had called my father a tyrant, yet for the most part his reign had been peaceful, Lord Gruffydd's only real failing being his reliance on indomitable will, yet wasn't that how all lordships and kingdoms ran? All the lands of Greater Brethon were bent under the rule of petty dictators and power hungry bishops who pressed the people down. The thought of it sickened me.

The darkness was complete when, at some unknown hour, I was pulled from a turbulent dream by the curious barking of a dog.

"Wha... who's there?" cried the guard snorting out of his semi-doze.

A friendly yip accompanied the clicking of paws and a small dog pattered up to the guard, who bent to wonder at this unexpected intrusion. "Hello, little fella. How did you get in here then? Did Gam bring you?"

Fussing over the dog, the guard failed to observe the shadow I noticed creeping along the wall. The shadow struck, followed by the sound of a scuffle and choking from the guard.

Then, like a song from heaven, a familiar voice said, "Mat?"

"Captain Beech!" I cried and instantly the stink of the dungeon was sweet as roses. "Please say I'm not dreaming. They told me you were killed."

"Not me, lad." With one hand, the Captain wrested the keys from the dead guard and unlocked the cell door. Taygan fussed around the Captain's feet. "Grand little distraction, this dog. Knows when to keep quiet and when not. I'm thinking of enlisting him in the militia."

Struggling to my feet, I saw a second masked man. "Who is this?"

"A friend. Come on lad, no time to dally," Captain Beech said, as his accomplice reached under my arm and supported my stumble to freedom.

Thus aided, I was hurried, limping down dim lit passageways, past two more bodies, before emerging into the courtyard under a moonless sky. Silently, we skirted the castle walls and crept out through the side gate near the latrines.

The masked stranger led us to a bend in the main castle road and gave a harsh bird call which was answered by the brief flash of a lantern from a coach and horses.

On nearing the waiting coach I pulled up short with a gasp.

"Captain!" I said, for I recognised the Skomer seal on the door.

The Captain urged me on. "Don't worry. She helped get you out."

"She?" My stomach lurched as the coach door opened and Morag waved us across.

The masked man climbed up to the driver's seat and took up the reins as the Captain and I got in.

I had little choice but once under way vented my anger at my traitorous cousin. "What manner of two-faced game are you playing, Morag? Does it amuse you to sport at my expense?"

"Sorry for what I did earlier, Mat. It was necessary." She didn't sound nearly halfway sorry enough.

"Necessary?! Your bloody husband damn near killed me. Where is he by the way?"

"Gone East with Sir Geraint. They're mustering troops to fight the Vukodlaks. The coast guards reported your boat's discovery to me. The man they killed was a known thief whom they assumed had stolen the boat until they found your belongings on board. They assumed you were in league. I have your possessions by the way, no need to thank me."

"Thank you? For rescuing me from the bloody mess you put me in?"

Captain Beech spoke across my rant, "She guessed what had happened and intercepted me at the old farmhouse. I was waiting until night settled before springing you."

"And you trusted her?" I said.

The Captain shrugged. "No reason not to, lad. Lady Morag has always been kind to me."

The coach rattled on through the night and I swore and cursed at every bump that jarred my bruised body. By the time we reached New Porth Clais, the moon had set and only the light of the harbour master's cottage pierced the darkness.

Pulling up the hood of her cloak, Morag stepped from the coach and knocked on the door. The harbour master appeared and the two exchanged whispers before he withdrew back inside.

Morag returned. "Your ship is ready to sail. Best you hurry, the tide is on the turn."

Glancing from the cottage to the masked coach driver, I said, "How many people know of this, Mog?"

"A few still loyal to the Pembrocks. Don't worry, I made sure I was safe from suspicion."

"Hugh could still find out," said Captain Beech.

"In truth, I don't expect him to return. If Hugh and his father think they can fare better against those creatures than Lord Gruffydd, then they are deluding themselves. I expect I'll be ruling here before long."

I frowned. "Is this what you've been working towards? First Lady of Neo Pembrock, not bowed by any Lord?"

"See, you are clever," said Morag, turning to smile as we hurried along the harbour wall. "Lady Constance always said you were. A very intelligent woman, your mother."

Limping as fast as I was able, I said, "Did you not wonder if I might want the title?"

"And do you?"

"No." I was certain of that.

Morag gave a sly grin. She had the better of me and I knew it.

Smiling I shook my head. "You're quite something, Morag. You know that? Listen, I tried to warn Hugh but he closed his ears, so I'm telling you. Ariadnii, the Spider Queen, is alive and far more dangerous than any Vukodlak. Come with us, it isn't safe for you here."

Morag shook her head. "No. I'm not yet ready to throw away what I've only just gained. Don't worry. I can evacuate to the quarantine isle of Rame if things get too warm. Brains over brawn, that's my strategy."

"It's not that simple. Ariadnii isn't stupid. Go to Eire. Start afresh."

Morag stopped and said sharply, "As what? Here I'm Lady Morag ruler of Neo Pembrock, what would I be in Eire?"

"Alive," I said.

Morag laughed. "Bless you, Mat. Fine. If it transpires there's no other option then I'll flee. Now board your boat and get out of here."

The craft moored to the harbour wall wasn't Dai's old crabber but I still recognised it. "Father Stephen's boat? You have a keen sense of irony, Mog. Did you rig it out especially for us?"

"Only one here without an owner, but yes, I thought it would amuse." She embraced me fiercely. "Take care of yourself, Mat. Perhaps one day we will meet again in better circumstances."

"And you, Mog. I don't have much of a plan at present but I have a few ideas. If they're successful I'll come and find you."

She laughed again but I sensed sadness behind it. "You are such a dreamer. I'm truly sorry I deceived you, Mat. Forgive me?"

"I'll think about it," I said with a smile, gathering Taygan in my arms.

With the wind picking up, I followed Captain Beech on board our vessel and cast off to catch the ebbing tide out into the channel.

A hollow sadness filled me as I watched the retreating shoreline. Hidden in the darkness were the rocks where Morag and I had watched the heretic come to shore. Too late, I remembered my ring, I could have given it to Morag, but the pact was broken so it might not have given the protection I would hope. I thought of Ma in Eire. I couldn't go to her, at least not yet. The bubble of faith my past life had been built around lay shattered in the dust of Llys Tywyll. I was the heretic now and the priests of Eire wouldn't welcome me. What had I achieved with all this folly? Nothing. The sense of failure tasted sour. I put a hand to my breast and felt the picture of Kazi and the Carringtons resting there. Suddenly, my heart was lit with revelation. Father Stephen's quest had come to nothing but he had burst the ties that bound me. I had outgrown my narrow life in Neo Pembrock. The world was full of mysteries to be uncovered and I had the drive and freedom to pursue them.

"Where we heading?" asked Captain Beech, his single hand resting on the tiller.

I looked to the guiding stars above. "To Free Kernow and after that who knows? We've a lot to discover, Captain Beech."

End of Book One